Quentin Blake's Magical Tales

Quentin Blake's Magical Tales

Written by
John Yeoman

PAVILION
CHILDREN'S

This edition first published in the United Kingdom in 2010 by
Pavilion Children's Books
an imprint of Anova Books Group Ltd
10 Southcombe Street
London W14 0RA

A CIP catalogue record for this book is available from the British Library

10 9 8 7 6 5 4 3 2

ISBN 9781843651550

Repro by Dot Gradations, UK
Printed by 1010 Printing International Ltd, China

This book can be ordered direct from the publisher at the website
www.anovabooks.com

Some of these stories have been published previously under the title *The Princes' Gifts*
(Pavilion)

Contents

Introduction

The little-known folktales I have brought together for this book come from very different parts of the world. But, for all that, they have a lot in common.

For one thing, when the stories were first invented they were intended to be told and not read. So they are all much, much older than the earliest versions that I have been able to find in books.

And for another thing, they all illustrate the element of magic which is such a familiar ingredient in most of the folktales that you got to know when you first began to listen to stories. Magic in all its weird and wonderful variations abounds in this book — in the form of wishes granted, supernatural powers, enchanted animals, transformations, the ability to fly, spells, visions, and all those other remarkable things that make folktales so vivid and exciting. The fact that, whether by coincidence or by direct borrowing, certain of the tales contain moments that remind us of more familiar stories only increases the pleasure, I think. For instance, we don't mind being able to

guess in advance that Aleodor's kindness to the three helpless creatures in *Half-Man-Half-Lame-Horse* will be rewarded handsomely in the end, just as will the young servant's to the old beggar in *The Magic Handkerchief* and the widow's to the old man in *The Pumpkin Tree*.

And I'm sure we all positively relish the age-old satisfaction of seeing the poor, simple characters turning the tables on the mean-spirited people who want to cheat them, as happens in *The Magic Cakes*, *The Witch Boy* and *The Magic Handkerchief*.

It is this marvellous mixture of the familiar and the unfamiliar, together with the colourful backgrounds of the stories, that will − I hope − make these magic folktales worth listening to and reading over and over again.

John Yeoman

The Blue Belt

In a far-off time in a far-off land there lived a young orphan lad who collected firewood from a nearby forest to make a living.

Late one afternoon, when it was beginning to get dark and his sack was still half-empty, the boy spotted a blue belt lying in the grass. He picked it up and tied it around his waist under his shirt. Suddenly he felt enormously strong, and knew it must be a magic belt. But he had no time to try its powers because it was getting very dark and he had to find himself a shelter for the night.

In the distance he spotted a glimmer of light coming from a tumbledown hut and decided to try his luck there. When he pushed open the door, to his surprise, there was an enormous troll sitting on the fireside bench.

"I've sat here for three hundred years" boomed the troll, "and never had a visitor yet. You'd better come in."

The lad sat himself by the troll's side and chatted away as if they were old friends.

"Might there be a bite to eat?" he asked, as bold as brass.

"If you're prepared to wait a while," said the troll, tossing six logs the size of young pine trunks on to the fire. And then, when the fire had settled into glowing embers, he rose and strode out of the house.

A few minutes later the door burst open and he came back in carrying an enormous ox on his back. He set it on the floor, felled it with one blow of his fist behind its ear, hoisted it up by its four legs on to the fire and turned it about in the embers until it was cooked brown all over.

He handed the boy a huge knife and invited him to help himself to the

meat, then watched in amazement as the lad carved off a thick slice the size of the table-top and gobbled it up.

"If you've had enough," said the troll, "I shall have a little bedtime snack." And with that he finished off the ox — hoof, horns and all.

But the troll wasn't as kind-hearted as he seemed. He was very offended that this slip of boy was so strong, and decided to teach him a lesson.

The next morning he said, "I would like to treat you to a drink of lionesses' milk for breakfast. There's nothing quite like it for a growing lad.

As it happens I keep a few lionesses in that further field. I can't milk them myself this morning as my back aches, so perhaps you'd could do it while I set out the breakfast."

The boy obliging took the pail and set off for the field. No sooner had he vaulted the hedge than twelve snarling lionesses appeared, twitching their tails threateningly. He marched over to the fiercest, bashed it over the head with his bucket and then swung it around by its tail until the terrified creature was yelping for mercy.

When he put it down all the others clustered around his feet like kittens, so he led them back to the troll's hut and left them at the door.

"I've brought the lionesses back with me," he called, "so that you can tell me how much milk we need."

"Nonsense," bellowed the troll from inside, angry that the boy hadn't got torn to pieces. "You haven't even been to the field!" And he flung open the door in a temper. Immediately the lionesses set upon him, biting and scratching until the boy had to speak to them very sternly and send them back to their paddock.

All morning the troll sat nursing his wounds and thinking how he could get even with the brat. And then he had an idea. His two brothers had a castle on the hill, and by that castle was an orchard where the most delicious apples grew. But anyone who ate even a small bite of one of those apples would fall into a deep sleep immediately.

"My brothers are ten times as strong as I am," said the troll to himself. "They will rip him apart as he sleeps."

"I really fancy some of those tasty apples from the castle orchard," he said to the boy. "But with my bad back... Why don't you pick a basketful for us?"

The lad was eager to help, but he was careful to collect the lionesses as he passed their field.

When they reached the orchard he climbed a tree and picked as many apples as he could, eating many along the way. But no sooner had he got down than a heavy sleep overcame him. Seeing this, the lionesses all lay down in a circle around him.

It was not until the third day that the troll's two brothers appeared, but they didn't come in the shape of an ordinary man; they came snorting savagely in the form of man-eating stallions.

At once the lionesses rose up against the troll-stallions, tearing them to pieces and finishing up every bit. When the lad awoke there they were purring contentedly around him and licking their chops.

Looking up he saw a pretty young maiden leaning from a window.

"You were lucky not to have been caught up in that terrible fight!" she called. "You would have been killed."

The lad tapped his magic blue belt. "I doubt it," he said.

Leaving the lionesses waiting patiently outside, he went into the castle to talk to the maiden. She told him she was the daughter of the king of Arabia and that the two trolls had kept her prisoner in the castle.

"And now I am free," she said. "What should I do? Shall I return home to my father or become your wife?"

"I'd love for you to become my wife," he replied. So they got married.

They lived happily in the trolls' castle until one day the princess felt she really ought to go back home to let her people know that she was safe and well.

"I'll tell them that I am married," she said, "and they will be sure to invite you to Arabia to join me."

So they loaded a ship and she set sail.

After a few months the lad was really beginning to miss his princess so he too set sail for Arabia, taking one of the trolls' giant swords with him.

The ship made good speed and he soon reached the city where the king of Arabia had his court. People everywhere were talking about how pleased the king was to have his daughter back again.

The lad stopped a stranger in the street. "Is it possible to see the princess?" he asked. "Does she ever appear in public?"

"No longer," said the man. "The king is given to strange moods and has hidden his daughter from all human gaze. But he has promised her hand in marriage to anyone who can find her."

'That is most unjust,' thought the lad. 'She is already married to me.'

Just then he noticed that one of the traders in the market was selling white bear skins. A plan immediately came into his mind, and so he bought a skin from the trader. He also bought himself an iron collar and a length of iron chain.

He explained his plan to his ship's captain, who was very willing to play his part. The lad dressed up in the white bear skin and the captain put the collar round his neck. Then he led him into the market place where he

danced and played tricks for the crowds.

People were so amused by the antics of the white bear that news of his success soon reached the king's ear. He commanded that the captain should bring his bear to perform before the court.

All the court ladies screamed when the captain first led him in, but the captain had his speech prepared: "The white bear is as gentle as a lamb," he reassured them. "He will only turn savage if anyone laughs at him. Please, no one laugh at the bear!"

The lad began his bear-like dance and all the company kept a very straight face but, at last, when he took the flute from the musician and began playing it himself, a waiting-woman couldn't restrain her laughter any longer.

Making ferocious noises, he lunged at her and ripped her beautiful gown to shreds so that she looked like a scarecrow.

Everyone fled the chamber, except the king.

"I like him," he said. "He must stay the night here in a room full of pillows and cushions."

So pillows and cushions were fetched and the white bear was put in the room to sleep alone.

At midnight the king came into the room with a lamp in his hand and took the bear by the chain. The lad was slightly puzzled but willingly followed him.

They passed through galleries and courtyards, they went upstairs and downstairs, they turned this way and that, until finally they reached a jetty which stuck out into the sea.

The king began to turn winches and haul on ropes, and work levers, until a little house rose up from beneath the water.

This was the house in which he kept his precious daughter hidden. Leaving the white bear outside, he went in to tell her about the surprise he had brought to make her happy.

"You call this a surprise, father!" she cried. "The creature will surely eat us alive!"

But the king explained that the bear was perfectly gentle unless anyone laughed at it, and brought him in. The princess managed to keep a straight face while the bear danced around the room, but when it put on the princess's head dress the waiting-woman burst into laughter.

At once the white bear pounced on her and tore her gown into shreds, and the frightened woman fled back to the palace with the tatters streaming behind her.

The king smiled. "I think the bear should stay here with you, my sweet, for the night." He was, indeed, a man of strange moods.

The princess didn't dare to protest, although she was frightened almost to death.

As soon as the door closed the bear rose and pointed to its collar. The princess understood that it wanted to be released, and unfastened the collar with trembling fingers.

Imagine her amazement when the lad slipped off the bear's head and spoke: "I've come to take you back."

When she recovered her voice she said that they must tell her father, for he would surely approve of the youth's enterprise.

"No," said her husband. "I must prove to him that I've won you fairly."

The next morning when they heard the sound of the winches and the ropes and the levers the princess replaced the collar and the lad curled up by the stove.

"I told you that you had nothing to fear, my dear," said the king as he led the white bear back to the palace, where he returned it to the captain.

Once they were in private the lad removed the bear-skin and went off to a tailor to order clothes fit for a prince. And when he was dressed in his finery he went back to the king and announced that he wanted to find the princess.

"Everyone is welcome to try," said the king. "But understand this. If you don't find my daughter within twenty-four hours you must leave the country immediately, never to return, and you must give up all hope of ever seeing the princess. Do you swear to this?"

It was hard, but the lad gave his solemn word.

He then surprised the king by saying, "Please summon the court musicians, your Majesty. I should like to begin with a dance."

The musicians came in, the court assembled and everyone danced and

sang for hours and hours.

"This is no easy task, young man," said the king. "And twelve hours have already passed."

"There's plenty of time," said the lad, and made the band strike up again.

Finally, "Go, pack your bags," said the king; "the time is nearly up."

"Light your lamp and follow me," said the lad. "There is almost one hour left."

To the king's amazement the lad followed the same way that he had led the white bear the previous night, though galleries and courtyards, upstairs and downstairs, turning this way and that, until they reached the jetty.

"It is no use," said the king. "This way leads only to the empty sea. The bell is about to strike."

"Five minutes to go," said the lad, turning the winches and hauling on the ropes and working the levers.

"The time *must* be up now," shouted the king.

"Two more minutes," said the lad. "If you'll pass me the key I'll have this door open in the twinkling of an eye."

"Ah, the key," said the king. "I quite forgot to bring any keys with me."

But the lad was still wearing his blue belt. "Then I'll have to open the door my way," he said, smashing it to splinters with the flat of his hand.

The princess rushed out into his arms, and the bell sounded. When the king heard that this was the one on whom his daughter's heart was set, he smiled on the couple and gave them his blessing. And that is the story of how a young orphan came to marry the daughter of the Arabian king.

The Five Strange Brothers

There was an old woman who had five sons who looked exactly alike. Nobody knew, but they were all strange. And what was most strange is that they were all strange in completely different ways. The first could swallow the ocean in one gulp; the second was tougher than steel; the third could extend his legs to any length; the fourth was unharmed by fire; and the fifth didn't need air to breathe.

The first brother earned his living by fishing. He worked by himself and amazed all the neighbours with the large catches of fish he brought home to sell.

Time and time again the townspeople would beg him to take their sons along with him on a fishing expedition, but he always made excuses. Finally, knowing how disappointed all the boys of the village were each time he refused, he agreed to take them — just once — on the condition that they do exactly what they were told.

When the day came, all the boys turned up early with their buckets and they marched behind him to the shore.

"The secret is to wait until the tide is right out," he told them. "Then you run out on to the wet sand and fill your buckets with fish. Once you have filled your bucket you must return to the beach and on no account must you take longer than half an hour. If you are in doubt, just watch me. I shall be sitting on that rock over there and I'll wave when it's time for you to run back to the dry sand."

Then he dived out of sight behind the rocks, drew in an enormous breath and sucked up the ocean for miles around.

The boys were overjoyed to see all the stranded fish flapping about on the wet sand and ran about scooping them into their buckets.

The first brother climbed up on to his rock to keep an eye on them and was very relieved to see how quickly they were filling their buckets. He knew that he couldn't hold his breath for more than half an hour.

But boys will be boys and as soon as they'd filled their buckets to the brim they started roaming further and further, inspecting shells, teasing crabs and having seaweed fights.

Time was passing and they showed no sign of returning. The first brother waved and waved, but no one was looking at him. He wanted to shout, but his mouth was full of sea water.

Finally, he had to give in. With a great gasp, he breathed out and the water gushed from him like a great tidal wave, drowning all the children.

Of course he had to go back to the village to report the accident and naturally all the parents were upset and angry. They hauled him before the judge.

It was no good the first brother explaining that he hadn't wanted to take the boys fishing in the first place, or that he had warned them not to disobey his instructions. The judge decided that he was guilty of murder and that he must be beheaded.

"I humbly accept your judgement," said the first brother, with bowed head. "But before I am executed, may I pay one last visit to my aged mother?"

The judge granted this request. When the first brother told his family how he had been sentenced to death, the second brother declared that they must do something about it.

"Change clothes with me," he said. "And I will go in your place. No one will ever know the difference." Reluctantly, the first brother agreed.

The second brother, now dressed like the first, knelt before the judge and thanked him for his kindness. Then he rested his head on the block.

The executioner raised his sword high in the air and brought it down with all his force on the bare neck. It rebounded off the flesh and sent the executioner sprawling on his back. He inspected the blade with disbelief: it had an enormous dent in it.

"I can't understand it, your honour," said the executioner. "This is our very finest sword, with a razor-sharp edge. I'm afraid I shall have to send to the prison for another."

"We cannot afford to spoil good swords on a murderer," said the judge. "The sentence will be delayed until tomorrow, when the culprit will be rowed out to the same sea which drowned his victims, bound with lead weight and dropped overboard."

"I humbly accept your judgement," said the second brother. "But before I am drowned, may I pay one last visit to my aged mother who thinks me beheaded by now?"

The judge granted this request, and when the third brother heard what had happened he suggested a plan.

"We can't give in now," he said. "Change clothes with me and I will go in your place. No one will even know the difference."

The third brother, now dressed like the first, was taken out to sea, weighed down with lead and thrown overboard.

As soon as he struck the bottom he extended his legs further and further until he was able to poke his head above the surface of the sea. Then, very slowly, because his arms were bound and he was weighed down, he began the long walk back to shore. He was careful, of course, to shorten his legs as he went, so that he just kept his head above water.

By the time he waded out of the shallows to greet the astounded judge on the beach he was back to his normal height.

"Shall we row him out again?" asked the villagers.

"Certainly not," said the judge. "We must use a method that will guarantee his death this time. Tomorrow he shall be boiled in oil."

The third brother respectfully begged leave to pay a last visit to his aged mother, who believed him drowned by this time, and his request was granted.

The fourth brother was quick to suggest another plan: "Change clothes with me," he said, "and I will go in your place. No one will ever know the difference."

When he presented himself, dressed like the first brother, before the judge, the oil was ready boiling in the cauldron. The executioner led him up the wooden steps to a platform above the boiling oil and pushed him in.

Not only did the fourth brother not scald to death, he swam around for a while and playfully splashed the terrified spectators.

"Take some ropes and fish him out!" thundered the judge. "If we can't execute him by beheading or drowning or boiling, then he will have to suffer the most terrible fate that our law allows: death by cream cake!"

The crowd gasped. It was indeed a terrible death.

All night long people were busy collecting and preparing the ingredients for the vast cream-cake: tons of flour for the solid pastry and cartloads of cream and sugar for the suffocating filling.

Meanwhile the judge was supervising the building of the enormous brick oven in which the cream-cake was to be baked.

"And to show you just how merciful I am," he said to the fourth brother, "I give you permission to pay one last visit to your aged mother who thinks you boiled to death by this time."

The fifth brother changed clothes with the fourth brother and reported to the mayor the following morning looking exactly like the first brother.

With the help of several oxen and good strong ropes, the executioner and his men dragged the cooked crust from the oven to the main square. The fifth brother climbed in and the execution team shovelled in the filling on top of him. When the master bakers had piped a little decoration across the top, the ceremony was declared complete.

"In three days' time we shall dig out his body," said the judge, "and return it to his family for decent burial."

As the pie filling was being scooped out on the third day, everyone was amazed to find the fifth brother very much alive, though slightly soggy.

"I can't tell you how glad I am to see you all," he said, climbing out of the pastry. "It was very dark in there and the cream was rather too sickly for *every* meal."

Having failed to behead him, drown him, scald him or suffocate him, the crowd agreed that all this had proved something – even if they couldn't quite decide what exactly! In any event, they felt that they had to ask the judge to pardon him.

The judge was only too ready to do so as he had had more than enough humiliation for one week. In fact, he went off for a rest cure and never returned.

The five strange brothers went back to live with their old mother and were never any trouble to anyone ever again.

The Magic Cakes

Many years ago, a long way away from here, there stood an inn next to a narrow wooden bridge across a river. No one who lived locally knew anything about the woman who kept the Footbridge Inn, except that she ran it by herself and seemed to be a widow.

The place always looked clean, the terrace was always well swept, and the only noise to be heard was that of the donkeys that grazed in the meadow at the back.

One day, a young merchant happened to be passing along that track on his way to the capital. As evening was beginning to close in, he thought he would stay at the inn for the night.

The landlady was most welcoming.

"I have five guests already," she said, "and so you will have company at supper this evening."

She fetched him a bowl of water to wash with, and then showed him into a room with a blazing fire where the other travellers had gathered to eat.

The meal was tasty and nourishing, and the guests soon felt relaxed and talkative. Some told of their adventures on the road, and others entertained the company with stories which they had picked up on their travels.

At last the young merchant found himself yawning.

"Please excuse me," he said, "but I set out very early this morning and must be up at cock crow tomorrow. I really think I should turn in for the night."

The other guests, all of whom had long journeys to make, agreed that this was a good idea.

"Respected gentlemen," said the landlady, with a charming bow. "Please allow me to offer you a glass of my delicious wine before you go to bed. I assure you that you will sleep all the better for it."

The young merchant politely declined, but the other guests thanked the landlady and drank to her good health.

Then she lit a lamp and showed them to the sleeping room on the floor above. There were just six beds in the room, and the young merchant took the one nearest the door.

In a very short while he could hear from their breathing that all his fellow guests were fast asleep. But for some reason – possibly he had eaten too much of the tasty meal – he lay awake.

And then he became aware of something moving stealthily on the floor below. Fearing that thieves might have broken in, he slipped noiselessly from his bed, opened the door a fraction and peered down into the lower room.

The landlady was crouching near the dying embers of the fire with a little box in front of her. She took a candle, lit it and then placed it in a candlestick on the beaten clay floor.

What happened next made the young merchant rub his eyes in amazement. She lifted the lid of the box and took from it first a little wooden ox, then a little wooden ploughman, and lastly a little wooden plough.

Then she gently raised a scoop of water from the water bucket, took some in her mouth, puffed out her cheeks, and sprayed the wooden figures with a fine mist.

At once they came to life. In the flickering light the young merchant could see the ploughman harness his ox to the plough and drive it backwards and forwards, furrowing the clay floor in front of the hearth.

When a space the size of a small mat had been ploughed, the landlady drew from her wrap a tiny quantity of seeds which she trickled into the little ploughman's outstretched palm.

He paced up and down the furrows, flinging the seed as he went.

Immediately green shoots of buckwheat began to spring up, and the grain began to ripen before the young merchant's astonished gaze.

The little ploughman harvested the grain, threshed it, ground it between two tiny millstones, and handed the flour to the landlady with a deep bow.

At this, the little figures turned back into wood again and she replaced them gently in the box.

The young merchant returned to his bed and lay awake all night thinking of what he had seen.

All the guests rose at dawn the next day and gathered their things together, ready for an early departure. There was a mouth-watering smell of fresh baking in the air.

"Respected gentlemen," said the landlady. "You would do me a great honour if, before setting out, you would taste one of my buckwheat cakes. I, too, was up early this morning, as you see. They are warm and fresh — and I made them especially for you."

All the guests bowed politely and accepted — except for the young merchant, who said courteously that he really had to be on his way.

"A thousand pities, gentle sir," said the landlady sweetly. "But perhaps you will pass this way again on your journey back from the city. And perhaps I shall be able to tempt you to a buckwheat cake then."

"It may be so," said the young merchant, and he settled his bill, bade farewell to one and all, and left.

But he didn't start his journey immediately — his curiosity was too strong. Making sure that no one could see him, he slipped over the rail of the footbridge, scuttled along the riverbank, and took up a position from which he could watch the back terrace of the Footbridge Inn.

He could hardly believe his eyes. Peering through the leaves, he saw the unfortunate travellers slowly turning into donkeys. First they sprouted long furry ears, then hoofs, then tails, then woolly coats, until they dropped on all fours, looking perplexed. Complete donkeys!

The landlady of the Footbridge Inn calmly ushered the meek creatures into her stables, before returning to collect all their baggage and taking it inside.

The young merchant was so worried that he clambered up on to the bridge again and hurried away as fast as his legs would take him.

His business kept him several weeks in the big city, but during all that

time he could not keep the donkeys out of his mind.

As the landlady had supposed, his return journey would take him past the inn again, and on the way he devised a plan.

On the morning before his arrival at the Footbridge Inn, he stopped at a village baker's shop and bought some buckwheat cakes that looked just like the ones the landlady had offered her guests. He didn't eat them. Instead, he put them in his shoulder bag.

He timed the last part of his journey so that he could arrive at the inn too late for a meal.

The landlady recognised him and was pleased to see him. His baggage was clearly bulging with goods.

"Respected sir," she said. "It is indeed an honour to welcome you again. Alas, I can offer you no company at supper this time as I have no other guests in the inn."

He explained that he had been eating, on and off, all day and would prefer to go straight to bed without any more food. He also declined the glass of wine she offered to him.

"Then you must have just one buckwheat cake with me," she insisted. "I should feel that I have not done my duty as your hostess unless I pressed you to take a little something."

"It is certainly not my wish to offend," he replied, bowing deeply, "but I can really eat no more today. However, nothing would give me greater satisfaction that to try one of your buckwheat cakes before I set out tomorrow."

The landlady looked extremely contented as she handed him the lamp for him to light his way to bed.

Once again he heard the faint noises from below. He did not look into the room this time but once again lay awake all night.

The next morning the air was filled with the appetising smell of fresh baking and a plateful of buckwheat cakes was waiting for him on the terrace table.

Making certain that the landlady was not about, he scooped the cakes on to a different plate and put the same number of cakes from his own supply on to the first plate.

A little later the landlady appeared.

"But you haven't eaten anything," she said, disappointed.

"Honoured lady" he replied. "Since you have been kind enough to offer your cakes, I hope you will accept my invitation to try some of mine, poor though they be by comparison." And he pointed to the plate of her own magic cakes as though they were his own.

She was only too willing to oblige him, and raised one to her lips with a smile, while he helped himself to one of the baker's cakes.

For a moment her eyes stared into his as she waited for the transformation to begin... but then her eyelashes grew longer and flickered, and her ears grew longer and twitched, and she turned into a gentle, but sturdy, donkey.

"I had better take the box of little wooden figures," said the young merchant to himself. "Although, since I have no idea how the magic works, I cannot lift the spell from the travellers."

But he did release all the donkeys into the meadows so that they would not starve.

Then he took a harness from the stables and fitted it on to the landlady-donkey. To his surprise, she proved to be very docile and very strong. He bundled his goods into side packs and set off back home at a much faster pace and in greater comfort than before.

For a few years the young merchant rode his donkey whenever he took a business trip. But one day, in a remote part of the country, he saw an old sage asleep on a stone bench by the wayside. As he drew up to him, the old man suddenly lifted his head and said, "Bless my soul, if it isn't the landlady of the Footbridge Inn!"

The young merchant was far too astonished to ask him how he could tell.

The old sage rose and patted the donkey's muzzle. "Young man," he said. "Your donkey has been good and obedient. These years of faithful service have surely made up for the wrong that was done. Let us set her free."

And with that he removed the bridle, and at once the donkey's form began to dissolve. The landlady of the Footbridge Inn stood before them.

To the old Sage she gave a deep bow, but to the young merchant she merely gave an empty look. Then she turned and walked away.

Nothing has been seen of her in that part of the world since.

Prince Baki and the White Doe

Once upon a time there lived a young king and queen who loved each other very dearly. Unfortunately, they were both very argumentative and were always having quarrels. Sometimes the king was right, sometimes the queen was right. But one thing was certain: neither of them would ever admit to being wrong.

One evening when they were reclining on their cushions after dinner, the king said, "Hush! Do you hear anything, my sweet?"

The queen listened for a moment and then smiled.

"I hear a fox in the palace ground, my love," she said.

"Not a fox, my precious," said the king. "A tiger. You can hear a big tiger roaring."

"I hear barking, my treasure," said the queen. "Tigers do not bark. That is a fox."

"This is really too much!" shouted the king, leaping to his feet. "I will not be contradicted all the time. Summon my counsellors immediately!"

The guards at the door ran off to carry out the king's command and soon the room was full of his wisest ministers and most senior advisers.

At a word from the king they all sat cross-legged on the floor and listened to what he had to say.

"You have been called to decide an important matter of state," said the king. "A little while ago, in the palace grounds, a creature began to roar..."

"Bark," said the queen.

"...and Her Majesty and I could not agree whether it was a tiger or a fox. If, in your wisdom, you decide that it was a fox, then I shall submit to being set adrift on a log on the great river that flows by our palace, to be taken where the current wills. If, on the other hand, you decide that it was a tiger – as I am sure it was – my adored partner will undergo the same fate. We leave it to your deliberations."

The queen was astonished to hear this and truly thought that her husband had gone quite mad.

Left alone to discuss the matter, the counsellors were of much the same opinion. But no one dared say as much.

"It is true," said one grey-bearded minister "That the barking was of a rather foxy kind... "

"And the pointed, bushy tail of the beast, which I happened to glimpse," said another, "was rather untiger-like..."

"Yet all the same..." continued a third.

"Yet all the same..." the senior minister interrupted. "If we say it was a fox we shall all be beheaded tomorrow. That confirms my opinion that it was definitely a tiger."

And so it was agreed. The king was so pleased to hear their verdict that he decided to be generous and give the queen one last chance. The next morning, as she placed herself astride the log, he whispered "Do you not think you might have been mistaken, my dear?"

"It was a fox," she replied, and pushed herself off from the bank.

After floating with the current for several hours, the log finally came to rest against some rocks on the further bank. The queen waded ashore through the shallow water and found herself among tall reeds and grasses.

A short distance ahead she thought she could see a wisp of smoke rising, and so she pushed her way towards it. There, squatting beside a small fire, was an old man with white beard down to his waist. He was cooking himself some food.

"Reverend sir," said the queen. "Please be kind enough to spare me a little of your meal. I have been travelling and am very hungry."

"I know," he replied, scooping some food on to a leaf and handing it to her.

"I am also lost," she said, when she had eaten.

"I know that, too," he replied. "But you will not be lost for long. You must follow that stony path to the top of the hill, where you will bear a child whom you must name Baki. He will not be like any ordinary child for, from the moment of his birth, he will be able to walk and talk. Great things are expected of him, and you must follow him wherever he leads."

The queen was amazed to hear all this but, thanking the old man kindly, she did just as he had instructed.

And, sure enough, she had a child on the top of the hill and the child immediately took charge of things.

"There is no time to lose, mother," he said. "Our destiny lies in that direction. Follow me." And he led her down the hill and through a wood and across a field.

"Let us sit in the shade of this tree," he said. "The princes will find us here."

Now the king of that country had three sons, and it so happened that they were out hunting that day and very shortly passed by the tree where the queen and her son were resting.

When the three princes heard the queen's remarkable story, they insisted on taking her and Baki back to the palace with them. The king bade his visitors welcome and not only offered them his hospitality but insisted that he should be allowed to bring Baki up with his own sons. The truth was that he was a widower, and much taken with the beauty of the queen.

Baki grew rapidly, and in no time learnt the skills of a prince. Soon he was more expert at hunting than his adopted brothers.

One day, when they were all four out hunting together, a beautiful snow-white doe broke loose from the undergrowth before them and bounded towards the mountains. They straightaway gave chase, but the going was rough and, one by one, the princes dropped back, leaving only Baki in pursuit. The poor doe herself was becoming exhausted now, and when she came to rest against the face of a cliff, Baki was confident that he had trapped her. But, to his amazement, she lightly touched the rock with her muzzle and it burst open, forming the entrance to a great cave.

As the deer leapt inside, Baki saw that it was suddenly transformed into a beautiful young woman. Without hesitating, he dismounted and slipped into the cave a second before the rock doors crashed together behind him.

Following the retreating form of the woman along winding corridors, he finally found himself in a vast stone hall, at one end of which were tall crystal columns.

"What ill-mannered creature are you that intrudes upon the privacy of a lady?" came a voice from behind him.

Prince Baki dropped on one knee before the beautiful young woman and swore that he meant no harm.

"And I hope that no harm befalls you," she said, in a softer voice. "For you are now in the hall of the most blood-thirsty ogre."

"But why are you here?" he asked.

She beckoned him to sit beside her on a stone bench.

"You must know," she explained, "that, like you, I am human. The ogre

34

took me captive some time ago and brought me here to wait on him. He hopes that one day I will agree to marry him – but I never shall. By watching and listening carefully, I have mastered some of his magic spells but I can never free myself from his while he is alive, and I cannot bring about his death on my own."

"Tell me what to do," urged Prince Baki, "and I will help you."

"That must wait until tomorrow," the young woman said, getting up. "I sense that he is approaching. If he finds you here he will tear you apart and eat you. This is the only place where you can hide."

She touched the central pillar and it swung open. Baki had only just climbed inside when the sound of crashing rock and footsteps echoing down the stone passageway announced the return of the ogre.

"I'm hungry," he growled. And then he sniffed the air.

"Human flesh!" he exclaimed. "There's been a human in here."

"It's your imagination," said the woman, making him sit down at the stone table. "See what a fine spread I have prepared for you tonight."

The vast meal put the ogre in a better mood, and when he had finished, he announced that he wanted some music.

Anxious to please, the lady took up her lute and began to play. Gradually, in time to the music, all the crystal pillars began to glide about in stately dance. All, that is, except the one in which Baki was hiding.

"What's this!" snarled the ogre. "It refuses to dance for me, does it? Then I'll crush it to splinters with my bare hands."

The lady was alarmed but her voice was calm. "My lord," she said. "The dance is in your honour. All the lesser columns pay their respect to the great and dignified central column."

The ogre was satisfied and smiled. In a good mood again now, he curled up in a corner and soon went to sleep.

The following morning he left, early as usual, but announced that he'd be back later to keep an eye on the cave, in case there was a human about.

As soon as he had gone, the lady released Baki.

"It is extremely difficult to kill an ogre," she explained. "His body is indestructible unless you can also kill his spirit. And his spirit is always hidden in some other object."

"And do you know where I can find his spirit?" asked Baki.

"Fortunately he talks in his sleep," said the lady. "Behind this cliff there is another tall rock that stands by itself. To enter it you must strike it three times with your right foot and each time you must say 'Great Raven, open the door.' At the third blow the door will open, revealing a great hall in the centre of which there is a red stone. On this stone is perched a green parrot. Kill the parrot and you will kill the ogre."

Baki kissed the lady's hand courteously and promised to do all he could to free her. She urged him again to take care.

Following her directions, he soon found himself before the standing rock. At the third time of his striking the rock with his right foot and calling, "Great Raven, open the door" a black shadow passed across the face of the cliff and the two doors flew open, revealing a dimly lit cavern.

In the centre of the floor a stone glowed red, and on that stone sat a green parrot. Prince Baki darted forward, seized it with both hands, and wrung its neck. At the very moment that the parrot squawked its last, there came a choked roar from the entrance of the cavern, followed by the sound of something very heavy falling to the ground.

Turning, Baki saw the dead body of the ogre sprawled across the threshold, his neck horribly twisted. His hand was still gripping a huge stone axe.

The lady greeted Prince Baki warmly, overjoyed that he had performed his task and had returned safely. Without more ado, the two of them set out on foot to the king's palace.

It was a long walk and the sun was hot and so, at the outskirts of the city, they stopped at an inn to take a bowl of tea.

They could not help overhearing the conversation of two travellers at the other end of the veranda.

"And has the king really passed the sentence of death upon the poor woman?"

"Indeed, he has," replied the other. "She has declined to marry him, saying that she already has a husband whom she loves, but the king is too enraged to listen to her pleas."

"If only Prince Baki were to return soon," sighed the first. "Perhaps he could help her."

"I doubt it," said the other, with a shake of his head. "The king, at heart, is a very selfish and cruel man."

And, fearing they had already said too much, they both fell silent.

Baki's feeling of triumph had turned to dismay.

"How can I save my mother?" he asked the lady.

"Not by doing anything rash," she replied. "The spells I picked up from the ogre shall not be wasted. All you have to do is leave me here a while at the inn, set out for the palace at once, and then..."

And she whispered into his ear.

Immediately Baki took his leave of her and hurried off to the palace. Without anyone seeing him, he slipped into the courtyard, sat himself down on the king's mounting block and muttered some words that the lady had taught him.

At once he was transformed into a large cowrie shell.

One of the guards passing by noticed the shell and strode over to take a closer look.

"That is a remarkably fine shell," he said to himself.

"Yes, I am rather handsome, aren't I?" Baki replied.

The guard leapt back a few paces in alarm. When he had recovered his composure, he approached the shell again.

"And what do you know about good looks?" he said sniffily. "You're only a cowrie shell, after all. You might be a talking shell, but you're still only a shell."

"I know more than you think," said Baki. "For instance, I know something about Prince Baki that the king would be very interested to hear."

Well, of course, when the guard heard this he ran straight to the Palace and told the High Chamberlain who immediately told the king.

At the king's orders, the cowrie shell was brought in and placed on a table before him.

"What's all this nonsense about Prince Baki?" he stormed. "Come on! What have you got to say for yourself?"

"Only this," said the cowrie shell. "If you try to marry Prince Baki's

mother or if you try to execute her, you will find yourself in great trouble."

"Threats!" bellowed the king. "From an impudent cowrie shell! We shall soon see who is in great trouble."

And, seizing a ceremonial sword from the wall, he brought the blade crashing down on the shell, smashing it into a thousand fragments.

Imagine the king's horror as he saw Prince Baki rise up before him and each of the shell fragments turn into a fully-armed warrior.

Seeing themselves so powerfully outnumbered, all the palace guards and the courtiers ran away to hide.

Baki's warriors spirited the terrified king and his sons to a castle at the other end of the country, where they were to remain prisoners for the rest of their lives.

Impressed by Baki's magical powers, all the ministers and courtiers and guards came to bow before him and begged him to be their king. Their work done, the warriors saluted king Baki and, turning into wisps of vapour, drifted up through the ceiling.

To everyone's delight, Baki took the beautiful young lady as his queen and they lived happily in the palace for several months.

Then, one day, Baki's mother made a suggestion:

"Your father has never seen his son, nor his daughter-in-law. And, for all his cantankerousness, I would dearly love to return to him. Could we pay him a visit?"

King Baki thought this was an excellent idea and plans were made immediately.

Once Baki's father had become used to the fact that he had a twenty-year-old son who was, in reality, only a few months old, he warmed to his new family. Of course, he was delighted to be with his wife again.

When the time came for Baki and his bride to return home, his mother stayed behind. She lived contentedly with her husband for the rest of their days.

And they didn't quarrel — well, not very often.

The Witch Boy

Many years ago a boy lived with his grandmother outside a village. They were very poor, but they were quite contented; the grandmother took good care of the boy, and he took good care of her.

The boy grew very fond of a girl who lived in the village. When she was grinding corn he would come to her window and talk to her, and she enjoyed his company.

But there was another boy who was also interested in the girl. He lived in the village too, and looked just like any ordinary boy, but he wasn't. He was a witch boy, and nobody knew.

He, too, used to visit the girl but, try as he might, he couldn't get her to say sweet things to him. She was always polite when he called, but it was clear that her heart was set on the other boy.

This made the witch boy very angry, and he decided to get rid of his rival. Pretending to be very friendly, he stopped to talk to him one day as the boy was collecting sticks for his grandmother's fire, and asked him if he'd like to go hunting.

"I know where there are plenty of rabbits," said the witch boy, "and I have a very special way of catching them which I'll teach you, if you like."

"That's very good of you," said the boy, not suspecting a thing. "There's nothing my grandmother likes better than rabbit for supper."

40

"I promise you she'll have her rabbit," said the witch boy. In fact, we'll probably catch so many that you'll have some to sell in the village. But, first of all, you've got to promise not to tell anyone what you're doing. It's a secret."

Of course, the boy promised willingly and they agreed to meet at a certain remote spot later that afternoon, at the time when the rabbits would be feeding.

They met at the appointed place, and the boy was eager to start.

"What's your special plan?" he asked. "Do we use a net?"

"Better than that," replied the witch boy, with a sly smile. "We change ourselves into coyotes by jumping over this," and he produced a small hoop from behind his back.

The boy looked rather doubtful, but the witch boy was very persuasive.

"No rabbit stands a chance against a coyote," he reasoned. "In no time we'll have as many rabbits as we can carry, and then we'll quickly change back and be home in good time for supper."

To show what he meant, he placed the hoop on the ground, jumped over it and immediately changed into a coyote. The boy did the same and was amazed to find that he, too, had changed into a coyote – with the tempting smell of rabbit in his nostrils.

Almost immediately he spotted a rabbit feeding a little distance away and gave chase. It took him no time at all to get used to hunting the way coyotes do, and it wasn't long before he had heaped up a tidy pile of dead rabbits by a rock.

Satisfied that the boy was too busy with his hunting to notice anything else, the witch boy jumped over the hoop, changed back into human shape again, scooped up some of the dead rabbits in his arms and, picking up the magic hoop, set off home.

The witch boy laughed out loud to himself as he trotted along.

"Not a bad afternoon's work," he chuckled. "Not only have I got rabbits for supper, but I've also succeeded in getting rid of my rival. The poor fool will have to stay a coyote for the rest of his days while I visit his girl as often as I please."

When the boy thought he had collected enough rabbits for the two of them he looked around for his friend and realised that he was nowhere to be seen.

At first he was puzzled. Then he began to get a bit anxious. And later, when it had grown dark and he couldn't find his friend — or the hoop — anywhere, he became seriously alarmed.

"What am I to do?" he wailed. "I can't stay like this!"

Meanwhile, his old grandmother waited and waited and worried and worried. She knew he was not the sort of boy to stay out without telling her what he was doing.

"Have you seen my grandson?" she asked a group of boys. "He didn't come home last night."

The witch boy was among them. He pretended to think for a while, and then said, "Ah, yes. I remember. I passed him yesterday afternoon. He said he was off hunting." And she had to be content with that.

For days and days after that the coyote boy roamed the scrub looking desperately for his supposed friend.

He was in a wretched state. He could not eat raw meat like real coyotes and he was afraid to try to light a fire in case the villagers saw the smoke and came to investigate, or set the dogs on him. In fact, he grew so weak and miserable that he would have died if the eagle spirits hadn't taken pity on him. From their place in the sky they had seen everything, and decided that the time had come to help.

They sent their swiftest eagle down to fetch him.

"Have no fear, young man," said the eagle. "We know that you became a coyote through trusting a false friend. Although your grandmother is now sick with grief and your false friend is singing his praises to your girl, all will be well. Climb on to my back. The eagle spirits are waiting for you."

The boy needed no persuading. He scrambled on to the eagle's back and found himself borne higher and higher, with the wind whistling through his fur.

Once landed, the eagle spirit led him into the Great House where the Chief Eagle was sitting in state. The hall was crowded with eagle spirits — men, women, boys and girls — all without their eagle feather coats, for they take them off and hang them on the wall when they are at home.

"Welcome to the village of the eagle spirits," said the Chief Eagle. "We shall return you safely to earth, never fear."

At a signal from the Chief Eagle, one of the eagle spirits fetched some hot water, while another dragged a large earthenware jar into the middle of the floor. The boy was lifted into the jar and the hot water was poured in. Then the Chief Eagle took a dried herb, the roots of which were in the form of a great hook, and twisted it into the coyote skin on the boy's head. Muttering some secret words, he gave a violent heave and pulled off the coyote skin in one movement.

The boy was his former self again.

The eagle spirit boys washed him all over and dressed him up in a splendid new outfit of soft buckskin and eagle feathers. Then the eagle spirit girls washed and combed his long hair until it shone in the firelight. After that they all sat down to a great feast that lasted, on and off, for four days.

At the end of that time, the Chief Eagle clapped his hands for silence.

"You have now grown strong and well again, young man," he said. "And so the time has come for you to return to your own people. You shall take with you not only our blessing but this deer which we have killed for you, and this herb medicine."

The eagle spirit men slung a deer across the boy's shoulders and fastened a small buckskin bag of herb medicine to his belt.

"Your false friend is no other than a witch boy," the Chief Eagle continued. "When you arrive he will be anxious to meet you, to find out how you changed back from a coyote. Say nothing, and behave naturally. Invite

him to a meal of freshly killed deer. And then, when he sits down to eat, sprinkle the herb medicine on his meat and justice will be done."

They helped the boy on to the eagle spirit's back again, and in no time he found himself among the rocks outside the village.

At his grandmother's house, he flung down the deer and cried, "Grandmother, I am back!"

When the old woman raised her head from her blankets and saw him standing by her side she almost fainted for joy. Although she had been very ill indeed for the past few days, the very sight of him soon had her on her feet again.

The news of his return spread quickly and, just as the Chief Eagle had predicted, the witch boy was the first caller.

"It is good to see you back, my friend," he said. "I was getting worried. You must tell me exactly what happened."

"I decided to hunt deer," the boy replied. "In fact, I caught a fine one and would be most honoured if you would join me in a feast tomorrow."

The witch boy couldn't understand but since his rival seemed so friendly and trusting, and since there was the prospect of a hearty meal, he accepted the invitation readily.

The following day the witch boy turned up in good time. The delicious smell of cooking that was hanging in the air put him in a very relaxed mood. He chatted away cheerfully to his host, thinking that he was an even bigger fool than he had first suspected. But he didn't notice the boy sprinkling a little of the herb medicine on his meat while he was pouring himself some water.

There was no immediate change. It happened gradually. First the witch boy found himself pushing his face into his plate to feed himself, then he realised he was lapping up water from the jug with his long tongue, and then he started scratching behind his ear with his foot.

"Oh no. I've turned into a coyote!" he would have cried, if he'd still been capable of human speech. As it was, all he could do was throw back his head and howl.

With no idea of what was happening, the grandmother rushed in and chased him into the street with her broom. Once the local dogs caught his scent they all came running, sending him fleeing into the distant scrub for safety..

The boy knew that all the dogs in the neighbourhood were first-rate guard dogs; they would never let a coyote anywhere near the village. And that meant that the witch boy would never be able to reach his hoop and change back into a boy again.

The boy went on visiting the girl until there came a time when they decided to get married. And then they both came to live with the grandmother and were all very happy.

In fact, the only thing that ever disturbed them was that sometimes, at full moon, they were kept awake by a lone coyote howling in the distance.

Half-Man-Half-Lame-Horse

A long, long time ago when bears had long tails and hawthorn bushes were covered with sweet pears, there lived an old Emperor.

His wife had died, and his pride and joy was his son Aleodor. The courtiers all agreed that it was only the old man's delight in watching Aleodor play, and hearing him chattering with the counsellors and the gentlewomen of the palace, that kept the Emperor alive for so long.

But finally the old man knew that his hour had come. He called Aleodor, now a young man, before him and made his last farewell.

"My son," he said. "There is nothing I can tell you about ruling these lands after me. From your tenderest years you have shown yourself to be wise and caring. But there is one warning which I must give you and which you must heed. Never set foot upon the mountain which you see in the distance. All the rest of these lands are yours, but that grim mountain belongs to the fearsome Half-man-half-lame-horse and no one who offends him lives to tell the tale."

Shortly after this the Emperor died, and while his people mourned the passing of the old man, they counted themselves fortunate in having the new young Emperor to rule over them.

Aleodor, by his thoughtfulness and fairness, fully earned the high esteem in which his counsellors held him. But not all his time was spent on affairs of state. In his spare moments there was nothing he enjoyed better than to ride his horse across the countryside and feel the wind blowing through his hair.

One day, however, he was galloping along with his mind on other things, when his horse suddenly neighed in alarm and reared up on its hind legs.

Too late, Aleodor saw that his way was blocked by the hideous creature known as the Half-man-half-lame-horse and he realised that he had strayed absentmindedly into the forbidden territory.

Aleodor was immediately filled with regret, not so much at what the foul beast might do to him but at having ignored the advice of his dying father.

"Villain!" snarled the Half-man-half-lame-horse. "What right have you to trespass on my property?"

"Please forgive me," said Aleodor calmly. "It was certainly wrong of me to enter your territory, but I beg you to believe that it was not done deliberately."

"A likely story," growled the monster, dribbling down its chin. "But, whatever your excuses, you are on my land and I mean to exact my punishment. You shall die like all the others." His claw-like hands began to twitch and his misshapen hind leg began to paw the ground.

Aleodor slipped nimbly from his horse. "I am not looking for a fight," he said, "but I am prepared to defend myself if I have to. Shall it be with swords, or clubs, or shall we struggle hand-to-hand?"

An evil glint came into the twisted creature's eye. "You are a foolish young man, but you do not lack courage. I might spare your life. Bring me the daughter of the Green Emperor within ten days and you shall go free. Otherwise, wherever you are and however closely you are guarded, be sure that my hooves will dash out your brains and my fangs will tear out your throat."

Aleodor felt that he had no choice, even if he also felt that he had little chance. He mounted his restless horse and, solemnly promising to perform the service in exchange for his life, galloped off along the track ahead of him.

After a while he found himself riding beside a lake and was surprised to see, a little way in front of him, a stranded pike thrashing around in the shallows.

Aleodor suddenly realised that he was feeling hungry and thought the pike would make a good meal. But as he dismounted to scoop it on to the shore, the pike spoke:

"Only spare my life, handsome youth," it said, "and I promise to do you as good a service in return." Aleodor felt pity for the stranded creature and lifted it back into the deeper water.

The pike twisted its body against a rock, dislodging a scale from its side.

"Take this scale," it said. "Whenever you look at it and think of me, I shall come to your aid." And with that, the pike plunged into the depths of the lake.

The young Emperor was travelling on, still lost in amazement at this strange encounter, when his attention was caught by a bird flapping helplessly in his path. He saw that it was a rook with a broken wing. "If I can't have a pike to eat," said Aleodor, springing down from his horse, "I suppose I must make do with a rook." At this, the rook stopped flapping and spoke. "Only spare my life, handsome youth," it said, "and I promise to do you as good a service in return."

Aleodor felt pity for the helpless creature, and gently straightened out its broken wing with a small splint made from a twig and a short length of creeper. He then lifted the bird to the safety of a dense bush. The rook flicked its tail against a branch, dislodging a feather.

"Take this feather," it said. "Whenever you look at it and think of me I shall come to your aid." And he disappeared into the leafy depths of the bush.

Aleodor travelled on, quite overcome with wonder at these two encounters.

Presently he heard the sound of running water and saw, just ahead of him, a small spring trickling from the rock.

"If I can't eat, at least I can slake my thirst," he said, preparing to dismount.

"Please take care!" came a tiny voice from below his right foot. If you put your foot on the ground you will crush me to death. Only spare my life, handsome youth," it continued, "and I promise to do you as good a service in return."

The young Emperor hastily slipped back into the saddle and peered down. He could just make out a little flying ant struggling in the mud, right where his boot would have landed.

Aleodor felt pity for the helpless creature and, easing the horse to one side, leapt down and rescued the ant by sliding a leaf beneath it. Then he shook the flying ant gently onto the grass by the path.

The ant scratched one of its wings against a little thorn, tearing off a tiny corner.

"Take this fragment of wing," it said. "Whenever you look at it and think of me I shall come to your aid." And it disappeared into the thick grass.

Aleodor, even more astonished, drank his fill, remounted his horse and continued along the track.

As night was falling, he found himself at the great gate in the wall surrounding the palace of the Green Emperor.

He knocked at the door and waited for someone to ask him his business there, but nobody came.

He waited there all night. He stood there all the next day; but nobody came. He stood there all the next day, but still nobody came. 'Time is passing,' he thought, with a heavy heart.

At dawn on the third day, however, the Green Emperor looked out from a window and thundered: "What kind of servants do I keep that they let a stranger stand night and day at my gates without asking him what he wants?"

The servants all looked ashamed and two of them were quickly dispatched to escort the stranger into the Green Emperor's presence.

"What do you want, my son?" demanded the Green Emperor. "Why do you wait so long at the gates of our court?"

Aleodor swallowed hard before he spoke. "I have come, mighty Emperor, to seek your daughter."

"Good," said the Emperor, smiling. "Very good. But first we must make a pact together, for such is our custom. You shall hide yourself wherever you think fit, three times. If my daughter finds you each time, your head will be struck from your body and impaled on a stake. Yonder you see that there is only one of the hundred stakes that does not yet bear a suitor's head. If, however, my daughter fails to find you, you shall receive her from me with my blessing. Consider carefully."

"I have considered," said the young Emperor. "Let us make our pact."

And so the deeds were drawn up and signed and sealed, and the Green Emperor summoned his daughter.

She stood looking at Aleodor for some time, and when she spoke there was no emotion in her voice.

"Hide where you will, young man," she said, "I shall find you. For I can see where no other human eyes can see."

The Green Emperor struck the ground with his imperial staff, at which all the members of the court melted away, leaving Aleodor to choose his hiding place. And all the time he was thinking about the ninety-nine heads on the ninety-nine stakes.

He explored the palace, he crept about the grounds, but every possible hiding-place seemed far too obvious. Just as he was about to give up in despair, he remembered his remarkable adventures on the road.

Sitting down on the rim of one of the garden fountains, he plunged his fingers into his pocket. He brought out the fish scale, placed it in the palm of his hand and conjured up a picture of its owner in his mind's eye.

Immediately the pike raised his head from the fountain pool.

"Tell me how I can help you, handsome youth," it said.

Aleodor explained his predicament and begged the pike to lend his assistance.

"I shall do what I can," he heard it say and before he knew what was happening he was borne away in a rushing of wind and a swirling of water.

When it was time for the Green Emperor's daughter to begin her search she stepped on to her balcony and looked to left and looked to right.

A puzzled expression crossed her face. "All the other unfortunates hid themselves in the cellars or in the barn lofts or in the haystacks," she said to herself. "But you have done something better than that, young man."

With this, she took her magic eye glass from around her neck and scanned the palace and grounds.

"Ah ha!" she cried at last, "I have found you; but I must confess you have given me much trouble to do so, for you have made yourself into a mussel lying on the sandy bottom of the sea." And she clicked her fingers.

At once the young Emperor was transported from his hiding place in the depths of the ocean and changed back into his human shape.

"You have found me at once," he said, and hung his head.

"Father," she said, "this youth is not like the others."

"We shall see tomorrow," said the Green Emperor.

The next day Aleodor slipped into the shrubbery and took the feather from his pocket. As soon as he began to gaze on it and think about its owner, the rook appeared on a branch above his head.

"Tell me how I can help you, handsome youth," it said.

Aleodor explained his predicament and begged the rook to lend his assistance. "I shall do what I can," the rook assured him. Aleodor then found himself being swept into the air and blown about the skies.

The Green Emperor's daughter stood on her balcony with her magic eye glass, scanning the palace grounds.

"Ah ha!" she cried at last, "Better and better, young man. So you thought to trick me by turning into a baby rook flying among the flock of rooks, did you?" And she clicked her fingers.

At once the young Emperor was transported from his hiding place in the air and changed back into his human shape.

"You have found me twice," he said, and hung his head.

The Green Emperor's daughter turned to her father. "Has the young man not shown remarkable skill?" she said.

"Indeed he has," he replied. "I long to know where he will hide himself tomorrow – for our contract says that he must hide, and you must find him, three times."

The next day, Aleodor slipped into a barn and delicately took the fragment of ant's wing from his pocket. As soon as he began to gaze on it and think about its owner, the flying ant appeared among the chaff on the floor.

"Tell me how I can help you, handsome youth," it said.

Aleodor explained his predicament and begged the flying ant to lend his assistance.

"There were only three chances, and today is the third and last," he urged.

"I shall do what I can," Aleodor heard the ant say, and then he found himself being blown across the barn floor and along the gravel paths.

The Emperor's daughter stood on her balcony with her magic eye glass, scanning the palace and grounds.

But she couldn't see the young Emperor. She peered far and wide, high and low, but still she couldn't see him. All day she looked, growing more and more bewildered.

Then, as the light was beginning to fade she came down into the garden where her father was waiting.

"I shall find him in a minute," she said. "I know he is near. Very near. But where exactly can he be?"

A gong sounded. Time had run out.

The Green Emperor smiled, pulled the contract from his pocket and solemnly tore it in two.

"Reveal yourself, young man," he said. "You have won our contest, and have won my daughter."

"Yes, reveal yourself," said his daughter, still amazed.

"Then kindly shake your skirts," came a small voice from somewhere near the ground.

The Green Emperor's daughter carefully shook the hem of her skirt and saw a tiny flower seed drop on to the gravel path.

Immediately Aleodor was changed back into his human shape.

"You didn't find me the third time," he said with a smile and looked her straight in the eye.

There was great rejoicing in the palace that night and great feasting. The Green Emperor would have ordered a month of celebrations, but the young man was so insistent that he must depart the next day that the Emperor had to agree to his wishes.

Before the assembled court he formally presented his daughter to the youth, and escorted them to the boundary of his empire with great ceremony. It should have been a moment of immense happiness for Aleodor, but his heart was heavy with grief at what was to come. He was a man of his word,

though, and had made a solemn vow to bring the Green Emperor's daughter to the Half-man-half-lame-horse.

The moment that the young Emperor had been fearing came when they stopped to take a drink at a clear spring. The Green Emperor's daughter put her arms around him and told him how relieved she had been that he had won the contest and had won her hand in marriage.

Aleodor released himself from her embrace. "Please find it in your heart to forgive me," he begged. "When I told your father that I had come to seek his daughter, I should have said that it was not for myself but for someone else." And he hung his head and looked wretched.

"If only you had told me so when I was at home," she said, with no anger in her voice, "I would have known what to do. But what's past is past and perhaps, even now, all is not lost."

They travelled on in silence after that until they came to the territory of the Half-man-half-lame-horse. As soon as he heard their horses approaching, he rushed out to claim his prize. Brave though she was, the Green Emperor's daughter hid behind Aleodor, while the deformed creature tried to induce her to go with him to his lair.

"For you are an Emperor's daughter," he slobbered. "And you shall be treated like an Emperor's daughter, my dear. You shall have fresh straw to lie on every fortnight and as many roots as you care to eat. Only let me hear you say that you'll be my loving wife."

She dropped lightly from her horse. With head held high, she said, "I know the man I desire to marry. If I cannot marry him I shall marry no one. And I shall certainly never marry you."

"You are making me angry, my dear," spluttered the Half-man-half-lame-horse, tottering from side to side in an agitated way. "And it doesn't do to make me angry, you know. You might regret it."

"I regret nothing," said the Green Emperor's daughter, taking a long branch and drawing a wide circle in the dust around her feet.

"Obstinate and strongwilled, are you?" snarled the Half-man-half-lame-horse. "Then I'll have to break your will. If you won't give me your hand, I'll just have to take it."

Aleodor was just about to leap down and attack the horrible creature when a look from the Green Emperor's daughter told him to hold back.

"We'll see who's strongwilled!" slavered the monster, hurling himself clumsily towards his prize.

But as he did so, the earth opened along the circle around the Green Emperor's daughter, forming a great gap that the spitting creature could not cross, no matter how hard he tried. He raved, he fumed, he screeched, until finally, so overcome was he with fury and shame that such a gentle creature should have got the better of him, he burst with rage.

The earth closed up, and Aleodor was able to reclaim his bride-to-be.

When his anxious people saw him returning safe and sound, they cheered as they had never cheered before. They took the radiant Green Emperor's daughter to their hearts and made her feel that she had truly come home.

The young Emperor and Empress soon produced a family, and it warmed the people's hearts to hear the sounds of young voices around the palace. And you can be sure that, though the distant mountain was now quite safe, no one ever set foot on it again.

The Magic Handkerchief

A long, long time ago there was a rich old miser and his wife who lived in the depths of the country. Although they were incredibly wealthy, they were also very mean and never gave anything to help the poor people around them.

For years they ran the house all by themselves, because they couldn't bear the thought of anyone seeing their possessions, and being tempted to steal them.

But one day the old woman sighed and said, "I sometimes think it would be nice to have someone to help me clean the silver and beat the carpets and prepare the meals. I'm not getting any younger"

Her husband looked up from the pile of coins which he was counting.

"I have been thinking the same," he confessed. "But think of the expense, and think of the worry of having a stranger in the house."

They both fell silent for a while. Then, at last, the wife spoke.

"Perhaps we could find some young orphan," she suggested. "She wouldn't need much to eat, and she could sleep in the stable."

"That's it!" said the husband. "She'd hardly cost us anything, and you could thrash her from time to time to remind her to be grateful to us for giving her a home."

And so, the very next day, the old miser rode off to the town and returned that evening with a young orphan girl. She was very frail and very frightened, but she was truly grateful that these people had taken her under their roof.

"Here's your supper," said the wife, handing her a bowl of stale rice and a mug of water. "And eat it slowly. We don't want you getting fat and lazy."

In the following months the girl worked from morning to night, with never a word of complaint. She polished the floors, washed the clothes, fetched the water, cooked the meals, and never had a moment's rest. At night, she slept outside in the stable.

Even the mean old wife had to admit to her husband that she was a treasure.

"The place has never been so clean and tidy" she said. "She doesn't cost anything to feed. What she eats is only what I'd have to throw away if she weren't here."

"That's true," said the old man, smiling. "But don't tell her how good she is, or she'll get conceited."

"Don't worry; I shan't," cackled his wife. "I still knock her head against the wall and pull her hair from time to time, to keep her in her place."

As the months passed, the poor servant began to grow weak and ill from

too much work and too little food, but still her master and mistress shouted at her for her laziness.

She took it all meekly and never complained. But deep down inside she was very unhappy.

One day, the wife said to her husband, "I've been noticing how beautifully our maid mends all the tears in her threadbare clothes. She's obviously a first-rate seamstress. If you took me to town I could buy some lengths of silk for her to make into gowns for me. Think of the money we'd save."

The husband agreed that this was an excellent idea, and so they set off immediately, leaving the girl a whole heap of jobs to do before their return.

As soon as they had gone, she looked at herself in the mirror and sighed at the change that had taken place.

Her hair was lank, her skin looked unnaturally pale and her hands were red and chapped. For a moment she felt like crying, but she pulled herself together and started to clean the pots and pans.

She worked and worked the whole day, without even stopping for a bite to eat, for she knew how angry the master and mistress would be if she hadn't completed her chores by the time they returned.

Her last job was to heat the stove. For fuel she had to use rice straw, and it usually happened that a few grains of rice would fall out of the straw when she took it from the basket.

Food was so precious to her that she used to pick up these grains and put them into a little bag. As she closed the bag she realised that she had enough now to treat herself to a bowl of freshly-cooked rice for a change.

A knock at the door made her jump. She immediately felt guilty, because she had been told time and time again that she wasn't to let anyone inside

the house when her master and mistress were away.

But when she half-opened the door and saw the stooping figure of an old beggar standing there, she immediately felt sorry for him.

"My kind young lady," he said in a cracked voice. "I haven't eaten all day, and am faint with hunger. Please ask your mistress if she could spare a bowl of food for an old man."

"Reverend sir," said the maidservant. "My mistress is not at home and I'm afraid that she would refuse you even if she were. But if this little bag of rice would help you, you are welcome to it, I'm sure. It's not much, I know." And she blushed with shame as she pressed the bag into his upturned palms.

In a voice that seemed slightly less quavery, the old beggar replied, "It is much more than I had reason to expect, my dear. I, too, have little to give. Only this handkerchief. You can use it when you wash your face. But be very careful not to let anyone else have it."

He bowed and walked away, with a spring in his step which surprised the girl.

She had no sooner tucked the crisp little handkerchief into her sleeve and turned to go back indoors when she heard her master's voice behind her.

"So that's what you get up to when we're away, is it?" he bawled. "Encouraging beggars and riff-raff!"

"You'll pay for it," said his wife, panting as she ran up beside him. "You'll go to bed supperless this evening. That'll teach you a lesson!"

The maidservant bowed meekly. It was no more than she was used to.

That night, alone in the stable, she dipped the handkerchief in her basin of cold water and wiped it over her face. It felt surprisingly refreshing.

Every night for a week, before she went to bed, the girl washed her face with the old beggar's handkerchief.

"I can't believe it!" gasped the mistress to her husband one morning. "Our maid has been transformed. Just look at her."

His wife was absolutely right. The girl's skin had a healthy glow, her eyes sparkled, her hair was silky, her hands were soft and elegant and she moved with grace and beauty.

"What have you been doing to your face?" the old woman demanded to know.

At first the girl couldn't think what she was talking about.

"Nothing," she said. "That is, every night I just wash it with a cloth

which the beggar gave me."

"Bring me that cloth," the old woman squawked. While the servant was fetching it the old woman turned eagerly to her husband.

"Don't you see?" she cried. "It must be a magic cloth that gives the user eternal youth and beauty. If we used it, we could become young again and lead a life of luxury for ever and ever!"

"Give me that cloth," the old man demanded, when the maidservant returned.

"I was told that I mustn't..." she began, apologetically.

"Don't argue with me!" said her mistress, snatching the handkerchief out of her hands.

Straightaway the mean old couple squatted down by a bowl of water and began to wash their faces and hands with the cloth.

At first, they were chuckling with delight, but after a while the old man said, "Doesn't it feel a little rough on your cheeks, my dear?"

The old lady agreed that it did.

"And the backs of my hands are feeling a bit itchy," she said.

"Mine seem to be getting uncomfortably hairy," said her husband, sounding very anxious indeed.

They loped over to the mirror to see what was happening and discovered, to their horror, that they had both turned into monkeys.

Gibbering and screeching with rage and humiliation, they bounded out of the house and off into the mountains. They were never seen again.

And the girl, a maidservant no longer, lived happily in the house on her own.

The Frog's Skin

Once upon a time there were three brothers who lived happily together. The brothers decided, eventually, that it would be a good idea to find themselves brides, but they weren't sure how to set about it.

At last, the youngest brother made a suggestion.

"Let us each shoot an arrow as far as we can," he said. "And from the place where the arrow falls we shall woo and win a wife."

The other two agreed that this was a good plan.

And so they took their bows out into the field. The eldest brother shot his arrow over the trees and set off to find it. The middle brother then shot his arrow over the trees and set out to find it. And, finally, the youngest brother shot his arrow over the trees and set out to find it.

The arrows of the two elder brothers had fallen in the grounds of noblemen's houses, and each of these two noblemen had a grown-up daughter.

The arrow of the youngest brother had landed by a stone at the edge of a lake, and on this stone there sat a frog.

The two elder brothers wooed and won their brides and brought them home in style. The noble maidens took to each other like sisters, but they were very upset when the youngest brother returned home with his frog.

At first things went well. The brothers went out to work and the two wives busied themselves about the house, making it bright and cheerful, and singing songs as they sat over their spinning and weaving. During all this time the frog crouched on the hearth, croaking.

But there came a day when the sisters-in-law grew tired of the sight of the frog.

"It does nothing but sit by the fire and croak," said one. "While we work hard to keep the home clean and tidy.

"And it stares at us so with its glittery eyes," said the other. "I'm sure it doesn't mean well."

They agreed to throw the frog out with the dust when they swept the house, and to say nothing about it.

But the frog just hopped back in again and took up its old position on the hearth.

Time and time again the sisters-in-law threw it out but every time it either hopped back in or waited on the path for the youngest brother to find it and place it gently on the hearth again.

Finally the two wives could stand it no longer and complained to their husbands.

"It isn't fair to us to expect us to keep company with a frog," said the eldest wife.

"If you truly loved us you would urge your brother to take a real wife, a nobleman's daughter," said the other.

And so the two elder brothers tried to persuade the youngest brother to get rid of the frog and find himself a more suitable wife.

But he was firm. "This frog is my fate," he said. "If I do not deserve better, then I must cheerfully accept what life has chosen for me and, above all, remain faithful."

At last his sisters-in-law grew so resentful that they insisted to their husbands that the frog must go.

"In that case," said the youngest brother when he heard the news. "I must leave too, and fend for myself in some other place."

With great sadness, he placed the frog in his pouch, said his good-byes and set off to make a new life for himself.

After a long journey he found an abandoned cottage and decided to settle there as best he could.

For a few days some of the neighbours would call in to lend him a hand, but when they saw the frog with its glittery eyes sitting on the hearth all the time, they thought better of it.

In the end, no one ever dropped by and the youngest brother had to put the cottage in order and till the ground all by himself. After the company he had grown so used to in his old house he felt very lonely. Now, when he came back from the field every evening to cook his meal, there was only the croak of the frog to greet him.

One day he came in from his work, tired and aching, to be greeted by an amazing sight. The floor had been swept, the table had been laid, and there was a pot bubbling on the stove. "Have my neighbours taken pity on me again?" he wondered. "Or have my sisters-in-law had a change of heart?"

The next evening there was a smell of freshly baked bread in the air to greet him and, again, a delicious meal had been prepared.

The evening after that, in addition to the meal, a bright cloth had been spread over the table and a jug of wild flowers had been carefully placed in the middle of the table.

'Whoever is doing this for me deserves my thanks,' he thought. 'Tomorrow I will see if I can catch them at it.'

The following morning he left the cottage early as usual but instead of going to the fields, he crept round behind the house and peered in at the window.

When all was quiet the frog leapt out of the fireplace and jumped all around the room to make sure that nobody was there. And then, to the youngest brother's amazement, it stripped off the frog's skin and emerged as a most beautiful maiden. She shook the skin and carefully spread it out on a stool before the fire.

And, then, in the twinkling of an eye, she swept and scrubbed and dusted, and prepared the food and cooked the meal, and made the place as welcoming as anyone could wish it to be. With that she moved gracefully back to the fire, slipped back into the frog's skin, and gave a contented croak.

The younger brother's head was spinning. He barely managed to get through his day's work.

When he returned that evening he greeted the frog affectionately, and placed it on the bench beside him while he ate.

He hid himself in the same way on the following day, because he had formed a plan. When he was sure that the beautiful maiden was occupied with her work, he rushed into the cottage and seized the frog's skin from the stool.

"Now you can be my wife for ever!" he cried in triumph. "I shall burn the skin and you will be free from the spell!"

"Oh, no!" she cried in alarm. "Please don't do that, I beg you. You don't understand – if you destroy the skin you might destroy yourself!"

But it was too late; in his excitement he had flung the skin into the fire where it blazed away to ashes in an instant.

"We were happy, in our way," said his wife quietly. "Let us hope that this one rash act has not turned our happiness to dust." And then, seeing how wretched he looked at her reproach, she kissed him sweetly and said, "And yet I know you did it out of love."

They spent the next months in great contentment and the husband never ceased to bless his good fortune. The news quickly spread that he had found himself a beautiful and sweet-mannered young wife and in no time the neighbours were calling in again to pay their respects.

Finally the lord of the country, a conceited and jealous man, came to hear of the marriage. "Why should one of my meanest subjects have such a gracious wife?" he said. "I shall take her for myself. Summon the peasant before us immediately."

The unfortunate young man listened with bowed head while the lord announced his intentions. It seemed as if his wife had been right and that he had brought a curse on himself when he burnt the frog's skin.

"But I am not an unreasonable man," the lord continued. "Perform three simple tasks to my satisfaction, and you shall keep your wife." He smiled.

"Sow a barn full of wheat tomorrow — that is your first task."

When the young man returned home he told his wife what the lord of the country had decided.

"All because I was reckless enough to burn the frog's skin I have lost you forever," he despaired, burying his head in his hands.

"What's done is done," said his wife. "That is the past, but tomorrow is the future. Perhaps we can do something about that! At daybreak you must return to the lake where we first met and call out, 'Mother and Father, I beg you, lend me your sturdy oxen.' Then lead them to the lord's fields and work them hard."

Her husband went to the lake's edge at first light and called, "Mother and Father, I beg you, lend me your sturdy oxen," and saw, to his amazement, a team of powerful oxen emerge from the lake.

The lord's barn was vast, but the oxen paced the fields without tiring from morning till evening, and the young man was able to complete the ploughing and the sowing in one day.

When the lord received the news he was most impressed, but even more determined to take the young man's wife from him. So he summoned him again.

"You did well on your first task. I grant you," he said. "But I doubt if you will find your second task quite as easy. Tomorrow you must go out and harvest all the wheat that you have sown, and fill my barn with it. But take care not to overlook a single grain, or else your wife is mine."

When the young man returned home he told his wife the new task he had to perform.

"It is impossible," he moaned. "I have lost you forever."

"At daybreak," said his wife, "go to the lake and call out 'Mother and Father, I beg you, lend me your sharp-eyed jackdaws.' Then take them to the lord's fields and work them hard."

Her husband went to the lake's edge at first light and called, "Mother and Father, I beg you, lend me your sharp-eyed jackdaws." To his amazement, he saw a flock of birds rise out of the water.

When they reached the lord's fields the young man discovered that overnight the wheat had grown tall and the seed had ripened. At a wave of his arms the jackdaws swooped over the fields, pecking the grain and carrying it off to the barn. All day they flew back and forth, without tiring.

But the jealous lord was determined not to be beaten, and had sent a servant out to see that every single grain was gathered from the fields.

As evening approached the lord stepped into his barn to survey the work. An angry look crossed his face when he saw that every space was crammed full of grain. But the young man was alarmed to see the angry look giving way to a smile when the servant ran in and whispered something in his ear.

"Just as I thought!" the lord exclaimed in triumph. "One seed short! My

trusty servant here reports that in the farthest field there is one tiny seed still not gathered."

At that moment there came a soft caw-cawing from outside and a jackdaw limped in, carrying a single grain in its beak. It was slightly lame and had only just reached the barn in time.

The jealous lord was furious. He resolved to set the young man a truly impossible task – one that he could never actually accomplish!

Turning to the young husband, he said, "You did well on your second task, I grant, but I doubt if you will find your third task quite as easy. My mother, when she died, took with her a precious ring which, by rights, should have been mine. Tomorrow you must journey to the other world and bring me back that ring, or else your wife is mine."

When the young man returned home he told his wife the new task he had to perform.

She looked serious. "This is, indeed, a near-impossible task. However, at daybreak, go to the lake and call out 'Mother and Father, I beg you, lend me your ram with the twisted horns.' Then mount its back and ride it hard."

Her husband went to the lake's edge at first light and called, "Mother and Father, I beg you, lend me your ram with the twisted horns." He saw, to his amazement, a huge ram rise out of the water. Its horns were twisted and its

mouth belched fire. Trembling in fear, he mounted on its back.

They flew across the earth like the wind until they reached the dark regions. On and on they travelled, the young man burying his face in the ram's fleece as they sped through the wall of fire, until they stopped before a sad-looking woman seated on a golden chair.

She looked at the young man and asked, "What can be wrong, my child? What brings you on such a dismal journey?"

In scarcely more than a whisper he told her how her son had sent him to collect the precious ring.

"My son is wicked," she said. "His wickedness must be punished. Give him this casket from me, but do not wait for him to open it." And she placed a small ornamental box in his hands.

The ram took him back through the wall of fire and the dark regions until they reached the fresh air and clear skies again.

As he had been instructed, the young man presented the casket to the lord, and left for home.

At first the lord was bitterly disappointed. But he was as greedy as he was jealous and soon reasoned with himself, 'I am receiving one priceless jewel in place of another priceless jewel; a fair exchange.'

With eager fingers he lifted the lid of the casket. At once there came a blinding flash of light and he disappeared off the face of the earth.

The young husband and his wife passed their lives contentedly in their little house and were never troubled again.

The Old Man and The Jinni

I n the far distant past, in a little village, there lived an old man and his
wife. He had worked hard all his life for very little reward, but now times
were hard indeed and he was often forced to beg.

To add to his misfortune, his wife, who had always had a sharp tongue,
constantly shouted at him and accused him of being lazy.

"You idle wretch," she shrieked at him one morning. "There's not so
much as a crust of bread in the place, and yet you never trouble yourself to
look for more work. Oh no! You couldn't care less if we starved to death!"

All this was untrue and unfair, but the old man knew better than to argue
with his wife.

"I'll see if I can find someone to hire me, dear," he said, as he left.

"Woe betide you if you don't!" she shouted after him.

But in the village no one would employ him; the harvest was finished and,
besides, he looked so frail.

And then a thought occurred to him. 'Why don't I journey to the town?' he asked himself. 'I shall never find work here, and my wife will only scream and shout if I return without a job. But in the town I might find someone to hire me.'

And so he trudged on towards the town, through the heat of the day. Just as he was becoming very thirsty, he saw a well shaded with trees a little way ahead.

He took a drink of cool water and settled down in the shade to rest his weary feet. But he hadn't been resting long before he saw a cloud of dust coming over the brow of the hill.

His heart turned to jelly. His wife was following him!

"Don't think I haven't been watching you!" she screamed, as she approached. "I saw you slinking off to the town to have a good time, leaving me to waste away without so much as a bone to gnaw on."

Instinctively he put up his arm to ward off the blows as she pummelled him about the shoulders with her fists.

But the ground was stony and uneven. She lost her footing and fell head over heels into the well.

'I must try to get her out,' thought the old man, in a panic. But then he reconsidered. 'Perhaps fate meant her to fall down the well and leave me free to find a new life in the city.'

And so, just in case fate should change its mind, he quickly set off along the track again. He hadn't gone far before he heard faint cries in the air and,

looking back, saw that another cloud of dust was approaching.

His heart sank. "I thought it was too good to be true," he said, preparing himself for the worst.

But it was not his wife. It was a jinni, and he was very angry. "I have come to slay you," he hissed. The old man fell to his knees. "Why should you wish to slay such a miserable wretch as me?" he quaked. In what way have I offended Your Greatness?"

"For fifty years I have slumbered peacefully in that well," boomed the jinni. "Until today, when you flung in that she-devil whose tongue is like a whiplash and whose voice is like the screeching of peacocks!"

"Then you should have mercy, O Great One," replied the old man. "Consider this – you have had fifty years of peace and quiet, and only one hour of my wife's scolding, but I have had fifty years of my wife's scolding and only one hour of peace and quiet. Surely I deserve your pity?"

"Your lot has indeed been hard," said the jinni. "But the fact remains that your wife is in my well."

"Then why not leave her there, and travel the world with me?" asked the old man, amazed at his own boldness.

The jinni was highly amused by the idea and agreed to accompany the old man to the town. He treated him to the best meal he had ever eaten in his life, and rented a large house with an army of attentive servants. Finding more gold is never a problem for a jinni.

For a few months they lived there happily but one day the jinni, with a serious look on his face, took the old man aside:

"We must part now, my friend," he said, "for if we continue to live together, I will surely do you great harm. It is in the nature of a jinni to make mischief and destroy happiness and I would not wish to bring further misfortune on a good friend."

"Alas," said the old man. "How shall I do without money?"

"I shall bestow a parting gift on you, in return for a promise," said the jinni. "And by that gift you will secure fame and fortune for yourself. It is my special delight to enter people's brains and drive them mad. When I leave you I intend to go to the capital and get into the brain of the daughter of the grand wazir. He is a very rich man, and desperately fond of his daughter, so he will give a generous reward to the person who can cure the possessed girl."

"And you will teach me how to cure her?" asked the old man.

"On one condition," said the jinni slyly. "You will never use this spell against me. I swear that if you do I shall enter your brain in revenge, and make the end of your days an absolute torment."

If you have any sense, you will never say anything to offend a jinni, and so the old man agreed to keep to the terms of the bargain. The jinni taught him the words of the magic spell and then disappeared.

It came as no surprise to the old man when he reached the capital to hear that the grand wazir's daughter had fallen seriously ill and that the wazir's own doctors had been unable to cure her.

The old man plucked up his courage and presented himself at the wazir's house, saying that he was a skilled physician from distant parts.

The wazir received him courteously but asked him if he really felt confident that he could cure a girl who seemed to be possessed by an evil spirit.

"I am absolutely confident, your honour, but I must demand a high fee for my services."

"Name it," said the wazir. "Our daughter is more precious to us than riches."

"My price is two thousand gold coins," said the old man.

"Two thousand gold coins!" the wazir roared. "That is outrageous! I shall try every physician in the country before I employ you. Be gone, and thank your stars for having got off so lightly for your impertinence."

The old man bowed and went away quietly.

The poor girl's condition grew worse, day by day. More doctors came and advised every different kind of cure. She had poultices laid on her brow, she was taken to the salt springs, she was anointed with balms and salves. But still she tossed and turned, moaned and raved.

The grand wazir sent for the old man.

"Cure her," he said. "I shall pay your price."

"Ah," said the old man. "My fee has increased, your honour. It is now one half of your possessions."

The wazir roared even louder than before. "Men have been whipped to within an inch of their lives for less than this! Remove yourself from my sight. There is yet a hermit from the hills. He shall cure my daughter, you rogue!"

The old man bowed and went away quietly.

The hermit was summoned, came, burned herbs and spices all about the room, and left the wretched girl ranting and wailing more feverishly than before. The grand wazir sent for the old man again.

"Cure her," he pleaded. "I shall pay you half of all I possess."

"Your honour," said the old man, "my fee has increased. It is now one half of your possessions and the hand of your daughter."

"I shall pay what you ask," said the grand wazir in a stony voice. "But see to it that the cure is perfect. If not, you can expect no more than a sound beating from my servants."

The old man was shown into the room of the wazir's daughter. It pained him deeply to see how the handmaidens had bound her tightly to her bed with cords of silk to stop her injuring herself.

Once he was left alone in the room with her, he whispered the magic words. Instantly she screamed and the jinni was expelled from her mouth as a puff of black smoke which disappeared out of the window.

The old man loosened the cords and led the smiling, grateful girl, fully restored to health, to where her father waited anxiously outside.

"This good man has delivered me from my prison of torment, father," she said. "He must be richly rewarded."

When the grand wazir explained what had been agreed, she said that she would be delighted to be the wife of such a man. And so all three were happy.

The old man and his new wife lived in luxury in one of the grandest houses in the city. As they sat, cross-legged, drinking coffee on their balcony one day, the old man said to his wife, "My life until this time had been one of perpetual misery, but now I see nothing but happiness before me."

He had spoken too soon. The grand wazir was announced and addressed his son-in-law courteously.

"The greatest of all honours is about to be bestowed on you," he said. "The khalifa has commanded me to take you to his palace, where his unfortunate daughter has just been possessed by a malicious spirit. The khalifa, in his generosity, grants you permission to cure her."

The old man was truly alarmed, for he guessed this was his jinni up to his wicked tricks again. If he refused to go to the palace, the Khalifa would punish him; but if he used the spell again, the jinni's punishment would be worse.

In the end, protesting that his skills were still imperfect, he allowed himself to be escorted to the palace.

"We grant you leave to cure our daughter at once," ordered the khalifa.

"My lord, I beg you to send for your court physicians first; my knowledge is very limited," stammered the old man.

"What!" thundered the Khalifa. "You cure the daughter of my grand wazir and, pleading modesty, you refuse to cure the daughter of the khalifa himself! Such modesty tempts the executioner's axe. You *will* cure my daughter!"

The wretched old man was taken under guard to the room of the khalifa's daughter and thrown in.

As he looked at her, he thought of the misery that he had brought upon himself, and a little tear ran down his cheek. Then suddenly his eyes lit up. His joints were weak, but his brain was still alert. "What an idiot I'm being," he said to himself. "Of course, there's a way out!"

Stepping closer to the bed, he boldly pronounced the magic spell. Instantly the daughter of the Khalifa screamed and the jinni was expelled from her mouth as a puff of black smoke.

But he didn't disappear out of the window. Instead, he hovered in front of the old man. "You old fool!" he hissed. "Don't say I didn't warn you. I was just settling down to a very pleasant time, tormenting this girl, but you had to spoil it. Well, you've asked for it. I am going to enter you now, and rack your broken body and brain for the rest of your wretched life."

"O Great One," said the old man sadly. "A few days ago, when I was truly happy, your threat would have terrified me, I have to confess. But now my wife has escaped from the well and has come to join me here. I fear you cannot make my wretched life any more wretched."

The black smoke turned decidedly pale.

"Your wife?" it gasped. "Escaped from the well? No, I'm not going to listen to her constant screeching and nagging! No, no! Anything but that!" And he swirled out of the window like a hurricane and was never seen or heard of in those parts again.

So the old man spent the rest of his days in contentment with his loving wife after all.

The Princes' Gifts

There were once three princes who were all great friends. Each of them was preparing to go on a long journey and, on the day before they set out, each chanced to see and to fall in love with a beautiful maiden looking out of her window.

The first prince, without telling the others, sent her a note saying that he must see her before he set out. She sent a note back to say that he might visit her at six o'clock, if he chose.

The second prince, without telling the others, sent her a note saying that he must see her before he set out. She sent a note back to say that he might visit her at six o'clock, if he chose.

The third prince, without telling the others, also sent her a note saying that he must see her before he set out. And she sent a note back to say that he too might visit her at six o'clock, if he chose.

When the hour arrived, the princes were upset to discover that the maiden had invited them all at the same time.

"It is clear that you care for none of us," said the first prince, "since you invited all three of us together."

"Not at all," replied the maiden. "I like all three of you very much."

"But you can only marry one of us," said the third prince. "Can you not tell us which one you will choose?"

"You are all so fine and charming," said the maiden, "that I cannot find it in my heart to like any one of you better than another. But since you must have an answer, I shall be happy to marry whichever one of you brings back from his travels the gift that pleases me most."

They had to be satisfied with that, so they thanked her kindly and took their leave.

A few days later, when they reached the crossroads where they had to part company, they wished each other well and agreed to meet at the same spot on their way home.

The first prince arrived at his destination and straight away set about finding a precious gift to take back for the maiden. One day, he saw a great crowd of people outside a glass-maker's shop and joined them to see what was going on. The glass-maker was holding up a looking glass and saying:

"This is a truly amazing looking glass. There is not another like it in the whole world. You have only to say to it, 'Looking glass, I wish to see such-and-such a person' and that person immediately appears, reflected in the glass."

The prince knew at once that this was the only gift for the maiden, and bought it for a bag of gold coins.

The second prince arrived at his destination and straight away set about finding a precious gift to take back for the maiden. One day he saw a great crowd of people outside a rug-maker's shop and joined them to see what was going on. The rug-maker was holding up a strangely-patterned rug and saying: "This is a truly amazing rug. There is not another like it in the whole world. You have only to say to it, 'Rug, take me to such-and-such a place' and it will instantly transport you there."

The prince knew at once that this was the only gift for the maiden, and bought it for a bag of gold coins.

The third prince arrived at his destination and straight away set about finding a precious gift to take back for the maiden. One day, he saw a great crowd of people outside a candle-maker's shop and joined them to see what was going on. The candle-maker was holding up a simple white candle and saying: "This is a truly amazing candle. There is not another like it in the whole world. You have only to place it between a dead person's hands and say

to it, 'Candle, bring so-and-so back to life' and that person will instantly be alive and well again."

The prince knew at once that this was the only gift for the maiden, and bought it for a bag of gold coins.

The day arrived when the three princes had agreed to meet at the crossroads. Each was eager to show his companions the wonderful gift which he had bought to win over the heart of the maiden.

The first prince held up his looking glass. "Prepare to be amazed," he said, and he commanded the glass to show him the beautiful maiden.

Imagine their distress when there appeared in the glass the reflection of the maiden, lying dead on her bed.

"All may not be lost," said the second prince, unfolding his rug. "Perhaps there is still a glimmer of life in her. I can transport us to her instantly and we can summon the best doctors to revive her."

He commanded the rug to take them to the maiden. No sooner had they stepped on to it than it rushed them through the air, and in no time they found themselves standing at her bedside. But it was clear that she was quite dead.

The third prince took his candle and placed it between her fingers. He then commanded it to make her alive and well. The maiden blinked her eyes, sat up, and smiled to see the three princes again.

"We are delighted to see you restored to life," said the third prince. "And since it was my gift that revived you, I beg you to remember your word and marry me."

"But it was my gift," said the second prince, "that transported us here, so I beg you to remember your word and marry me."

"But it was my gift that told us that you were dead," said the first prince, "so I beg you to remember your word and marry me."

"You all three have my undying gratitude," said the maiden. "And you all three have a claim to my hand. But since I cannot marry three husbands, I shall not marry any of you."

The beautiful maiden went away to shut herself up in a tower. And the three princes, sadly disappointed, did exactly the same.

The Crystal Ship

A long time ago there lived a merchant who had three daughters. One day, when he was about to set out for a distant country on business, he thought he would ask his daughters what they would like him to bring back for them.

His eldest daughter said, "If you please, father, I should like a beautiful silk dress."

His second daughter said, "If you please, father, I would also like a beautiful silk dress."

His youngest daughter couldn't think of what to ask for at first. Then her mother whispered in her ear: "Say you would like the Jewel-of-jewels."

"If you please, father," said his youngest daughter. "I should like the Jewel-of-jewels."

The father loved his daughters very dearly and promised to bring them back the presents they had asked for.

He travelled by ship to the distant country where he had dealings with many foreign merchants, and when his business was over and it was nearly time to leave he went to the market. There he bought two wonderful dresses of the finest silk, and hurried back to the harbour to catch his ship home.

The ship was ready to set sail, but the captain came up to him, looking very serious, and said, "Have you completed all your business here, sir? Are you sure that nothing has been left undone? For my ship cannot sail if there is someone on board whose work is not completed."

The merchant slapped his hand to his forehead and exclaimed, "I had quite forgotten my promise to my youngest daughter!"

The captain begged him earnestly to do what he had promised, for otherwise the ship could not move out of the harbour.

The merchant hastened to the street of the jewellers and asked who could sell him the Jewel-of-jewels.

"No one," he was told. "The Jewel-of-jewels is the name of the son of the Sultan of the Jann."

The merchant was determined. "Where might I find him?" he asked.

The jewellers told him how the reach the Sultan's palace and smiled to themselves as the merchant set off on his quest.

He found himself at a gate in the wall of the palace, and knocked boldly.

A voice from behind the wall asked him what he wanted.

"I am looking for the Jewel-of-jewels," he replied.

At that the gate was opened and there stood before him the most handsome youth he had ever seen.

"I am the Jewel-of-jewels," he said. "What do you want with me?"

The merchant bowed, and answered, "I have promised to return home with presents for my three daughters. To the two eldest I promised silk dresses; to the youngest I promised the Jewel-of-jewels."

"You shall not break your promise," said the youth. "When you return home you must build a room and leave it empty. Take this box. It contains three hairs. Give it to your youngest daughter and tell her to sit all alone in the

empty room and rub the three hairs together. But warn her that on no account must she cry out in alarm at what she sees. Instead she must simply say, 'This is my fate' and all will be well."

The merchant took the small box from the youth, made another deep bow, and returned to the ship.

When the oldest daughter unwrapped her new silk dress she was delighted and thanked her father warmly. When the middle daughter unwrapped her new silk dress she, too, was delighted and thanked her father warmly.

The youngest daughter waited patiently for a while and then asked, "And have you brought back a present for me, father?"

The merchant was troubled in his mind about the little box and replied, "I am sorry, my dear. I quite forgot what it was you asked for and so have brought you nothing."

That night he sought his wife's advice. He told her that the Jewel-of-jewels was the son of the Sultan of the Jann and explained about the box and the room.

"I do not know what is for the best," he said. "Should we build the room or not?"

"We must build the room," said his wife. "And good fortune will follow."

And so the room was built and left empty. On the day that it was finished the mother and father led their youngest daughter to the room, placed the box in her hands and told her how to rub the three hairs together.

"But on no account, my dear, must you cry out at anything you may see. Only say, 'This is my fate' and all will be well."

She was quite afraid, but assured her parents that she would do just as they had instructed her. They then left her alone, locking the door behind them.

She sat on the floor and took the three hairs from the little wooden box. Then she started to rub them together gently, all the time staring at the closed door.

Soon she became aware that the floor beneath the door was turning into a lake, and that a ship made of purest crystal was floating through the door, and that on this ship was the most handsome youth she had ever seen.

"This is my fate," she said, quietly.

The young man, smiling, stepped down from the crystal ship and embraced her. They instantly fell in love with each other and contentedly

passed the hours in gentle conversation.

When it was nearly time to leave, the youth said, "If anything should ever happen to part us and I am unable to visit you here, you must go out into the world and seek me – if you truly love me. But you must be sure to put on shoes of iron and carry a staff of iron."

With that he kissed her goodbye and sailed away on his crystal ship.

Her anxious parents were relieved to see their youngest child so happy when they unlocked the door the following morning. But she told them nothing about the Jewel-of-jewels.

Many, many nights she spent in perfect contentment with her visitor until her eldest sister became so tormented by curiosity that she devised a plan to discover the secret.

One afternoon when the mother took the three sisters to the town baths the eldest sister pretended to be feeling suddenly unwell.

"It is nothing, mother," she said. "I am just feeling a little faint. While you bathe, I shall sit outside in the fresh air and I will quickly recover."

She waited until they had undressed and gone into the baths, and then took the key of the room from her sister's pocket.

Back home, she let herself into the room and found the little wooden box. At first she was disappointed to discover that it contained nothing but three hairs and turned them over between her fingers in disbelief.

But, of course, as she accidentally rubbed them together the floor became a lake and the crystal ship sailed into the room.

The eldest sister was so startled that she cried out in panic. At once the crystal ship burst into splinters, many of which pierced the body of the Jewel-of-jewels, before the vision disappeared and the room became a room again.

Frightened and guilty at what she had done, she ran back to the bath house and quietly returned the key to her youngest sister's pocket.

That evening when the youngest sister went to the room and rubbed the three hairs nothing happened. She sat there through the night softly crying to herself, but brightened when she thought of what could be done.

The following day she went to her father and mother and told them that she must have a pair of iron shoes and an iron staff. As they were so sorry to see her unhappy, they had them made for her immediately.

She travelled and travelled through deserts and through valleys, until she came in sight of a walled city. Her feet were sore and tired from the long journey, so she sat down to rest in the shade of a tree.

In the branches of the tree were two doves cooing to each other, and although they were talking in dove-language she could understand everything they said.

"If the maiden's asleep, she's fated to weep,"she heard one of them coo.

"If the maiden can hear, she need have no fear,"cooed the other in reply.

The first dove continued, "Can this be the maiden beloved by the son of the Sultan of Jann? The maiden whose sister stole the key and caused the crystal ship to burst into splinters?"

"It is, indeed," replied the other. "The splinters pierced the body of the handsome youth and now he is grievously ill. His father seeks everywhere for a medicine to cure him."

"And there is only one,"said the first dove. "If the maiden is awake and listening now, she will know how to come by it."

"She must first kill us and collect our blood and feathers and take some leaves from this tree," said the second dove. "Then she must go to the Sultan of the Jann disguised as a physician who has the skill to cure the boy."

"Then she must have him taken to the baths," said the first dove. "She must anoint his body all over with our blood and feathers to make the splinters of crystal fall out."

"And after that" said the other, "she must wipe him all over with a handful of leaves. Then the youth will be cured."

At this the doves dropped lightly to her feet. She wrung their necks, slit their throats, drained their blood into a bottle, plucked their feathers and tied them in her handkerchief, before stuffing a handful of leaves into her pocket. Then she set off for the city.

She went first to the bazaar where she bought herself a long cloak with a hood, and then she went to the palace of the Sultan of the Jann where she introduced herself as a skilled physician.

The Sultan of the Jann was so desperate to save the life of his beloved son that he willingly accepted the help of this stranger.

"First, you must have your son taken to the hot baths, and then you must leave him there with me until I call you," said the youngest sister.

"It shall be done," said the Sultan of the Jann. And so the almost lifeless youth was carried to the hammam, the hot baths of the city, undressed, and laid out on a marble slab.

When she was alone with him she took the feathers, mixed them with the doves' blood, and smeared the mixture all over his body. As she did so, she could hear the splinters of crystal falling on to the marble floor. Then she wiped his skin clean with the leaves, and his wounds closed and healed so perfectly that there was no blemish to be seen.

He woke with a start, saw a hooded figure bending towards him out of the swirling steam, and thought for the moment that he must be dead.

But when she pulled back the hood and smiled at him he realised that this was his loving companion whom he had visited so often in his crystal ship and he knew that she had saved his life.

"I put on shoes of iron and carried a staff of iron and came to find you, Jewel-of-jewels," she said.

"Then you truly love me," he replied, and embraced her tenderly.

When the Sultan of the Jann was summoned, and saw his precious boy alive and happy again, words could not express his joy or his gratitude.

No matter that the young woman had deceived him by pretending to be a physician, he said she had done him the greatest service he could ever demand and he would give her the greatest reward that she could ever demand.

And he was overjoyed when she said, "The greatest reward would be to give me Jewel-of-jewels as my husband."

The wedding was arranged and people came from miles around to wish the young couple well and they lived in perfect happiness ever after in the country of the Jann.

The Pumpkin Tree

There was once a poor widow who had six hungry children to feed. Early every morning she used to sling a sack over her shoulder and go out looking for something to eat.

One day, she saw a very old man sitting on a log by the river.

"Good morning, mother," said the old man.

"And good morning to you, father," said the widow.

"If you have a little time to spare, would you be kind enough to wash my hair for me?" asked the old man.

Well, the widow didn't really have much time to spare as it took so long to collect roots and berries to feed her hungry family. But she felt sorry for the poor old man, so she said she'd be pleased to wash his hair for him.

When she had finished, he thanked her very kindly and held out a small coin. The widow hesitated. "You don't have to pay me," she said. "I was pleased to be able to help you."

"Do your children like pumpkins?" asked the old man.

"My children love pumpkins," said the widow.

"In that case," said the old man, "take the coin and walk along that path there. After a while you'll come to a tall tree covered in pumpkins. It's a magic pumpkin tree. Dig a small hole at its root and bury the coin there.

Then, whenever you want any pumpkins, just call for as many as you like."

The widow told him how grateful she was, and trotted off along the track.

There, sure enough, was the tall pumpkin tree covered in pumpkins. She got down on her knees, scrabbled away some loose earth, and buried the coin. Then she stood up to think what to do next.

"I mustn't be greedy," she told herself. "I'll ask for just enough pumpkins to keep the children well fed and happy."

So, "Six pumpkins, please," was what she said.

To her delight, six beautifully ripe pumpkins floated down and landed gently at her feet. She gathered them into her sack and hurried off back home. There she boiled the pumpkins and sat down with her children to the best meal they'd ever had.

And every morning she was able to leave enough boiled pumpkin to keep the children contented until she returned from her work.

One day, to her surprise, she found a baby on the doorstep. "The poor little mite looks hungry," she said. "It will be no trouble to care for it and feed it — as long as it likes pumpkin."

So the good-hearted soul changed her request to the magic pumpkin tree. "Seven pumpkins, please," was what she said now.

After a while she began to notice that all the boiled pumpkin had been eaten up and the pot licked clean when she returned from her work. And yet her children were still hungry.

"But I left you enough boiled pumpkin," she said.

"We know," they replied. "The baby eats it all."

"The baby!" she exclaimed. "That's nonsense; a little baby can't eat all that much boiled pumpkin."

"We know," they said. "But, all the same, he does."

The widow made a plan. The next morning, while the baby was still asleep in his cot, she sent the children to play in the fields.

Then she rigged a big wicker bird trap above the pot of pumpkin.

If anyone touched the pot, the trap would catch him. She was a wily old widow.

Later, when she came back to the hut with her children, she heard a howling and a bawling.

"Let me out! Let me out!" It was the baby, caught in the trap.

"I'll let you out — and turn you out," said the widow, hauling the baby out of the trap. "There's gratitude for you, trying to eat me out of house and home. I've a good mind to give you a smacked-bottom!"

But she never did because, to her amazement, the baby suddenly turned into a hefty young man with a very disagreeable look on his face.

All the children hid behind their mother's skirts as the brawny fellow snorted in annoyance and stormed off towards the river. There he came across the very old man.

"What's all this about a magic pumpkin tree?" demanded the bad-tempered young man.

"Ah, the magic pumpkin tree," sighed the old man. "I don't suppose you have time to stay and wash my hair for me, do you?" he asked.

"Whether I have the time or not, I don't intend to do it," shouted the young man, with an even more disagreeable look on his face. "Just tell me where the magic pumpkin tree is."

The very old man pointed a gnarled finger at the path, and the young man tramped off without so much as a thank you.

When he reached the magic tree, he gazed up at the plump, ripe pumpkins with greedy eyes.

"Now, one would probably be enough to be going on with," he thought. "But why leave so many on the tree, tempting other people to steal them from me? No, I think I'd better take ten."

So he looked up into the branches of the magic pumpkin tree and yelled,

"Ten pumpkins, and be quick about it!"

And, sure enough, ten pumpkins came hurtling down on his head and crushed him to death.

The Three Old Crones

There was a princess who was deeply in love with a prince. He was also deeply in love with her and told her that he would ask permission of his mother, the queen, for them to get married.

When she heard her son's request the queen frowned: "I refuse to allow my son, the heir to the throne, to marry an idle girl," she said. "When I was young I was praised for my spinning and weaving and sewing – your bride must be equally skilled. Is she?"

The prince had to confess that he did not know, but felt sure the girl he loved must be skilled. He pleaded so desperately that the queen seemed to relent a little.

"Very well," she said. "Since you are so confident I shall invite this king's daughter to stay with us here. Then I shall give her some simple tasks so that she can prove how nimble her fingers are."

The prince was delighted. The princess, although she did not show it, was dismayed. She had been waited on all her life and no one had ever shown her how to make herself useful with her hands.

The queen greeted her coolly when she arrived. "You shall be taken up into the maidens' bower," she said. "You will find all you need there. Tonight you will be given a pound of flax, which you must spin before dawn if you wish to marry my son. And be sure that the flax is spun as finely as I used to spin it."

With a sinking heart the princess followed the servant up to her room in the maidens' bower. As the door closed behind her and she was left all alone she sat on the window seat and sobbed into her handkerchief.

Unexpectedly there came a little cough from behind her and, turning, she saws the tiniest little old woman with an enormous pair of feet sticking out from under her cloak.

"Peace be with you, child," said the little old crone. "May I ask what makes you so unhappy?"

"Peace be with you, too," replied the princess. "I have good cause to be unhappy: unless I spin this pound of flax before dawn, I can never marry the prince."

"If that is all, you can dry your eyes," said the little old crone. "My name is Mother Bigfeet. I shall spin the flax for you, never fear."

The princess was overjoyed and begged the little old woman to tell her what she would like in return.

"Very little, my child," she said. "The honour of being invited to your wedding would suffice. You know, I have not been to a wedding since the queen was a bride."

The princess willingly agreed to the bargain and the little old crone slipped out of the room. She had a very troubled sleep that night and was already wide awake at first light when the little old woman crept back into the room and pressed a bundle of yarn into her hands.

"Well? What do you think of that?" she chuckled.

"It's as white as snow and as soft as a cobweb," said the princess. "It's beautiful."

"As beautiful as the yarn I spun for the queen before her wedding. But that was a long, long time ago," said the crone and slipped away again.

Shortly after, the queen arrived and inspected the yarn. "It is certainly very fine," she said frostily. "I wonder if you will do as well with tonight's task."

The princess was anxious all day and felt even more so when it was time to return to the maidens' bower.

"Tonight you will weave this yarn into the finest tissue. You will find everything you need in your room. If you wish to marry my son, be sure that the task is finished before dawn and that the tissue is woven as finely as I used to weave it."

Alone again in her room, the princess sat down on the window seat and began to cry.

Another little cough made her turn, and there she saw the tiniest little old woman with an enormous bottom sticking out behind her.

"Peace be with you, child" said the little old crone. "May I ask what makes you so unhappy?"

"Peace be with you, too," replied the princess. "I have good cause to be unhappy: unless I can weave this spun flax before dawn, I can never marry the prince."

"If that is all, you can dry your eyes," said the little old crone. "My name is Mother Bigbottom. I shall do your weaving for you, never fear."

Again the princess was so relieved that she begged the little old woman to name a price.

"All I ask is the honour of being invited to your wedding. You know, I have not been to a wedding since the queen was a bride."

They made their bargain and the little old crone slipped out of the room.

The princess was wide awake when the little old woman crept back into the room and draped the cloth over her hands.

"Well? What do you think of that?" she chuckled.

"It's purest white and as smooth as delicate skin," said the princess. "It's beautiful."

"It's as beautiful as the tissue I wove for the queen before her wedding. But that was a long, long time ago," said the crone and slipped away again.

When the queen appeared she was so obviously impressed by the fineness of the weaving that the princess hoped that there would be no further tasks. She was quickly disappointed.

"Well and good so far," said the queen in an icy tone. "But I doubt you will find tonight's task so easy."

That evening the poor princess learnt that she was to make the cloth into shirts for the prince, and that – if she wished to marry him – the task had to be finished by dawn.

The princess could scarcely believe her eyes when a third little old woman slipped into her room. On her right hand she had the most enormous thumb.

She, too, comforted the princess and assured her that the work would be done well before the appointed time.

"My name is Mother Bigthumb," she said. "I will make the shirts for you. All I ask in return for this favour is the honour of being invited to your wedding. You know, I've not been to a wedding since the queen was a bride."

The princess was overjoyed and gave her word. Early the next morning the little old woman presented her with the shirts.

"Well? What do you think of these?" she chuckled.

"The stitching is so neat and delicate. I have never seen anything like it" exclaimed the princess. "The sewing is really beautiful."

"It's as beautiful as the sewing I did for the queen before her wedding. But that was a long, long time ago," said the crone before she slipped away again.

The queen could barely conceal her anger when she came to examine the handiwork.

"Who would have thought you were as clever as that," she said. "Well, take him then!" And she slammed the door behind her.

The king was very pleased when he was told that the wedding of the two young people was to go ahead. He had grown very fond of the princess.

For days, the prince and princess planned and made arrangements for the big day. They were both very excited but the princess couldn't help thinking about the three old crones and their invitations to the celebrations.

There was music and dancing in the great banqueting hall and everyone was wishing health and happiness to the young couple. The princess kept peering into the deepest corners of the hall but try as she might, she couldn't see her strange little guests anywhere.

"And now, my dears," said the king, standing up. "I think we should go round the company saying a word or two to all these good people." And he led the way.

At last, they found themselves facing the three tiny old women, seated together round a table tucked into a dim alcove.

"I've never seen these strange creatures in my life," the king whispered to his son. "I'm sure I couldn't have invited them. How embarrassing. Still, we mustn't be discourteous. They obviously mean no harm."

The first old crone rose to her feet and made a deep curtsey. "My name is Mother Bigfoot," she said. "I have such large feet because so much of my time is spent spinning."

"Is that so!" said the king. "Then my son's wife shall never spin another thread!"

"My name is Mother Bigbottom," said the second. "I have such a big bottom because I sit weaving for so much of my time."

"In that case," said the king. "My son's wife shall never weave again!"

"And my name is Mother Bigthumb," said the last crone. "I have such a big thumb because I have had to do so much sewing in my time."

"Then my son's wife shall never sew another stitch!" said the king.

The prince and the princess lived very happily together, and the queen never again criticised her daughter-in-law.

As for the three crones, people say they were sometimes spotted sitting together in a shady corner at big weddings.

The Poor Girl and Her Cow

T here was once a couple with one child, a daughter. They loved her very dearly and when the mother got very ill and was about to die, she called her daughter to her bedside.

"I am leaving you my cow," she said, squeezing her hand. "Love her and take care of her, and she will be very good to you."

Some time after the mother died, the father married another wife who already had a daughter of her own. The two little girls grew up together but the new mother resented her husband's daughter and was always finding fault with her.

But the girl did not complain. As her mother had advised her, she loved and tended her cow and was happy to spend hours in her company.

The cow was indeed good to her. The girl discovered that if she gave her raw cotton to eat, she would return it a little later neatly spun and finely woven.

Every day the girl would take her into the scrub at the edge of the desert and get her to spin and weave cotton.

The jealous stepmother used the girl's absences as an excuse to make trouble: "That daughter of yours never lifts a finger about the house," she complained to her husband. "All she does is day dream with that cow in the

desert. You must have that cow killed; there's nothing else for it."

The husband thought this was very unreasonable, especially as his stepdaughter sat around the house eating all day.

"The girl is not getting up to any mischief," he said. "And however much she day dreams, she still spins and weaves plenty of cotton. As for killing the cow, why, it was left to her by her mother! No, the cow shan't be killed."

His wife frowned, but let the matter drop.

One breezy day when the girl was in the desert, two lengths of cotton which the cow had spun and woven were blown away and the girl ran off to catch them.

They were blown past a water channel and into the cave where a hairy old water witch sat milling flour between two stones. She had her back to the entrance and didn't hear the girl approaching.

The girl was so starved by her stepmother that she couldn't resist the temptation to help herself to the witch's food. She scooped up a little of the flour and popped it in her mouth and washed it down with a sip from the water-flask that hung at the witch's back.

As soon as she realised what was happening the old crone turned round and said: "If I had seen you before you tasted the flour and the water I would have swallowed you whole. But as it is you are now my daughter. Let us sit at the mouth of the cave. I feel awfully sleepy. I'll put my head in your lap so that you can catch the lice – and be sure to eat any that you can find."

The girl did not like the idea of this, but didn't dare to protest.

"Above all," said the water witch. "Remember this rhyme:"

Water white, give me a call,
Water yellow, give me a call,
Water black, say nothing at all

And she fell asleep with her head in the girl's lap.

The girl couldn't slip away, and so she had no choice but to remove the lice from the old witch's hair.

And what disgusting creatures they were! Fat ones, thin ones, crawly ones, wriggly ones, soft ones, crunchy ones.

Just to keep the old woman happy she picked up a few grains of corn that were lying around and from time to time cracked one between her teeth.

"Yum, yum," she said. "What delicious lice you have, mother."

Very shortly she noticed that the water in the channel was beginning to run white. Remembering the witch's instruction, she tapped her on the shoulder and told her so.

"Go into the water and wash," the witch commanded.

The girl did as she was told and when she came out she was as fair as the morning and her skin was as soft as silk.

The water witch put her head back into the girl's lap and the girl picked more lice from her hair.

Then she noticed that the water in the channel was beginning to run yellow. Remembering the witch's instruction she tapped her on the shoulder again and told her so.

"Go and dip your head into the water," the witch commanded.

The girl did as she was told and when she came back her hair was as golden as the corn and so long that it reached right down her back.

But she was afraid at what her stepmother might say when she got home, and told the water witch.

"Bind up your hair in this cloth, and your step mother won't notice a thing."

The girl smiled and thanked the witch.

"But for all that, she will kill your cow."

The girl began to cry, but she still listened to the witch's words.

"All will be well, but on no account eat of her flesh. Put the bones and skin and all that remains into a bag and bury the bag at a place where she spins and weaves the cotton. Leave the bag buried for forty days and then dig it up again. Whatever is in the bag will be yours."

And so the girl left the water witch, returned to her cow and drove her home with a heavy heart.

"She has gone too far this time," complained her stepmother when her husband came in. "She stayed out the whole day, enjoying herself goodness knows where. And it's always the same excuse – she's looking after that pampered cow of hers!"

Her husband tried to reason with her: "She is very fond of the cow," he said. "And however much time she gives to it, she still spins and weaves her cotton beautifully."

Said the stepmother icily: "Enough is enough. Either you go out and kill that cow this very minute, or I leave this house."

The father was kind hearted but weak. He went out and slaughtered the cow. He skinned it and cleaned it, then threw the remains into the yard.

The stepmother and her daughter had never looked happier than they did when the supper was ready.

"Take your fill, everybody," said the stepmother. "It was a lazy beast when it was alive, but it'll make some tasty meals now that it's dead."

The girl pushed her plate away and refused to eat any of it. Instead, she went into the yard and put the skin and bones and head and tail and all the other remains into a bag and ran out into the desert, where she buried everything. When she came back she sat in a quiet corner and wept for the death of her cow.

One bright morning when nobody was about she unbound her long, golden hair and washed it. Then she went up on to the roof to dry it and comb it out in the sun.

But the stepmother happened to see her and was amazed at the sight.

"How did you come to have such beautiful silken hair?" she demanded.

And the girl had to explain how she had followed the two lengths of cotton into the water witch's cave.

"That's just like you," shouted the ill-tempered woman. "Keeping all the good things to yourself. Well, you can go right back to the water witch's cave and tell her to make my daughter's hair even more beautiful than yours!"

She called to her daughter to stop eating and go with her stepsister, and to be sure to do exactly what she was told.

"You'll have to keep reminding me," the stepsister grumbled as they went out to the desert. "I can't be expected to remember everything for myself."

As before, the water witch was in her cave, making flour. The girl made her sullen stepsister understand that she had to pop a little flour into her mouth and wash it down with a sip from the water flask that hung at the witch's back.

"If I had seen you before you tasted the flour and water I should have swallowed you whole," said the witch, when she realised what had happened. "But as it is, you are now my daughter."

Then, just as before, she invited her visitor to pick the lice from her hair while she had a little sleep.

"Do as she says," whispered the girl to her reluctant stepsister.

"And, above all," said the water witch in a sleepy voice. "Remember this rhyme:"

Water white, give me a call
Water yellow, give me a call
Water black, say nothing at all

"How I am supposed to remember all that?" grumbled the girl, beginning to run her fingers through the witch's hair. And then she saw the lice and threw up her hands with a scream.

"I am not going to do this," she shouted. "She'll just have to give me beautiful hair without this. I refuse — I'm going to wake her."

She tapped the witch on the shoulder. "Wake up," she said and pointed to the channel, quite forgetting what she'd been told. "Look — the water is running black."

The witch roused herself. "Go and dip your head into the water," she commanded.

When she was gone the water witch turned to the girl and said, "Did I not tell her to do nothing if the water ran black?"

The stepsister returned in floods of tears. There were two enormous black horns on her head and she was even more ugly than before!

The mother was even angrier when they returned home, even though she knew it was really her own daughter's fault.

The days passed and on the fortieth the girl slipped away into the desert and unearthed her bag. Imagine her delight when she opened it to find that the skin had become a richly embroidered cloak; the tail had become an elegant silk dress; the bones had become jewelled bracelets and necklaces and rings, and the hoofs had become a pair of clogs, set with diamonds and emeralds.

She put on her finery and went to admire herself in the brook. Then she hid the clothes in the bag again and decided come back to the spot so she could try them on every day.

One day when she was splendidly dressed and twirling around to catch the breeze in her long golden hair, the son of the sultan happened to be riding along the crest of the hill.

For a time he watched her in admiration but suddenly, sensing that she was not alone, she hastily hid the finery away in the bag and ran off home. In her haste, she dropped one of her clogs into the brook.

Immediately the sultan's son sent one of his attendants down to find it. He was sorry to have lost her, but was determined to find her again with the help of the jewelled clog.

Back at the palace he confided in his mother, and told her how much he wished to marry the owner of the clog.

"Good, my son," she said. "But we must not alarm the gentle creature. I shall find her myself."

His mother took a handmaiden and travelled far and wide in search of the girl with the golden hair, but could not find her anywhere! Few girls had such hair as her son had described and the little clog would fit none of them.

Finally, only one house remained to be visited. "We shall surely find my son's bride here," she said.

The jealous stepmother had heard that the wife of the sultan was looking for a bride for her son and had bought her daughter the most expensive clothes she could afford. But however thickly she draped the silk headscarves over her head, it was impossible to conceal the horns completely.

"I won't have you standing there and looking shabby," she snapped, rounding on her stepdaughter. "Get into the oven and don't you dare make a sound!"

They were not baking, so there was no fire under the oven but it was still an uncomfortable place to be. The poor girl curled up as tightly as she could but the space was so small that she couldn't get her feet in properly.

But the stepmother had no time to deal with that because the wife of the sultan had arrived:

"My daughter and I are honoured to receive such a gracious visitor in our

humble abode," said the stepmother, hastily adjusting a headscarf over one of the horns.

"Have you no other daughter?" asked the sultan's wife.

"This is my only daughter, my pride and joy," said the woman.

At that moment the girl in the oven, who couldn't hear what was going on and had no idea that the visitor had arrived, called out, "I'm afraid my feet are sticking out!"

"Who is that?" asked the sultan's wife.

"I heard nothing," said the stepmother, looking flustered.

"I'm afraid my feet are sticking out!" came the voice again.

"The voice appears to be coming from the oven," said the sultan's wife.

"It's the cat, then," said the step-mother hurriedly. "It's always getting into the oven."

"I'm afraid my feet are sticking out!" came the voice yet again.

The sultan's wife crossed over the oven, saw the little feet, and signalled to her handmaiden. The handmaiden knelt before her with the jewelled clog on a small embroidered cushion. The sultan's wife looked from the feet to the clog and then to the feet again.

"Pray, come out of the oven, my dear," she spoke.

Despite the stepmother's protests, the sultan's wife insisted that the girl should try on the clog. And, of course, it was a perfect fit.

"I shall take you with me to the palace," said the sultan's wife in a kindly voice. "I will introduce you to my son."

The young people fell in love with each other instantly, and the sultan and his wife were so happy for the young couple that they ordered a grand wedding celebration that lasted seven days and seven nights.